SO-BIH-873

STRINGS ATTACHED

STRINGS ATTACHED

•

Amanda Harte

AVALON BOOKS
NEW YORK

PRINTED IN THE UNITED STATES OF AMERICA
ON ACID-FREE PAPER
BY HADDON CRAFTSMEN, BLOOMSBURG, PENNSYLVANIA

For Diane Thomson,
critique partner *extraordinaire*, with heartfelt thanks for your
encouragement and especially for the times when you said,
"This could be better."

Chapter One

If she hadn't been so angry, she might have laughed at the sheer absurdity. After all, how often did you find a woman who had just inherited a million dollars sitting by the side of the road in a broken-down car? She should have been riding in a private jet or, at the very least, a chauffeured limousine. But no, Rachel Fleming was driving her own, third-hand Mustang when the engine clanked, whooshed, and then stopped, leaving her ten miles from her destination.

So much for her plan to sweep into Canela, her head held high in an imitation of bravery she was far from feeling. Now she'd be lucky to limp in, if she made it in at all today. A ten-mile walk in ninety-plus degrees was hardly a stroll in the park. Only a fool would even attempt it, and whatever else she might be, Rachel was no fool. She tied a scarf to the outside mirror to alert passersby to her problem, locked the door, cranking the window down an inch for ventilation, then closed her eyes as she settled in for a long wait.

"Lady, do you need help?"

The man tapped on the window, repeating his question. Rachel's eyes flew open, and for the briefest of moments she was disoriented. Then memory washed over her. Grandma's will. Danny. The car.

"Do I ever!" She unlocked the door and slid out, brushing her long blond hair away from her face. "The car just stopped," she explained with a disgusted glance at the engine.

"Let me try."

Rachel tried not to wince. The man couldn't help it that he was the epitome of everything she'd tried to leave behind. Tall and lean, he wore faded jeans, an equally faded chambray shirt, scuffed boots, a Stetson, and an expression that said if he didn't own the entire state of Texas, he ought to.

"Go ahead." Who knew? Maybe a cowboy was what the Mustang needed. The man climbed into the car and turned the key. Rachel held her breath. Maybe, just maybe, a miracle would happen. It didn't. The engine screeched for the cowboy just as it had for her. But unlike her, he wore a confident grin as he walked to the front of the car. After a moment spent communing with the mysteries of the internal combustion engine, he closed the hood, and gave it a gentle pat.

"It's the water pump." The man's blue eyes were solemn as he delivered the verdict. "I'm afraid your car's not going anywhere under its own power."

"This is definitely not my day." Miracles, it appeared, were in short supply in east Texas.

"If you don't want to wait for the tow truck, I can give you a ride to the next town." He gestured toward the big red truck parked on the other shoulder. Its water pump was obviously still functioning, for Rachel could hear the engine idling.

"I'm going to Canela."

The man grinned again. "Then you're in luck. That's where I'm heading. I can drop you anywhere in town you want." With chivalry that Rachel had thought extinct, he opened the passenger's door and helped her climb into the truck.

It was cool, blessedly cool, and for a second Rachel did nothing more than enjoy the air conditioning. Then she said, "There used to be a gas station on the south end of town. If it's still there, they probably have a tow truck."

It had to be a trick of the light that the man's lips appeared to twitch as though he were trying to control a smile. After all, there was nothing amusing about gas stations and tow trucks.

"Station's still there," he said. "Sounds like you've been to Canela before. You visiting friends in town?"

Rachel grimaced. If only it were that simple. "I'm going to be living there."

Though she tried to keep the rancor from her voice, apparently she did not succeed, for he gave her an odd glance. "It's a good town," he said as his eyes moved slowly, seeming to catalogue her features and assess her clothing. So what if her skirt was short? She had chosen it deliberately. The man's lips twitched again, and Rachel wondered if that was a silent commentary on her shocking pink toenails, but he said only, "I moved back about six months ago."

Rachel looked at him more closely. He was probably her age, maybe a year or two older. It was hard to tell with the Stetson still shadowing his face and hiding most of his hair. He didn't look like anyone she remembered from the years she had spent in Canela, but then she hadn't tried to keep those memories alive. In all likelihood, the man had lived there during the thirteen years she'd been gone.

"I used to live in Canela, too," she volunteered, "but I have to admit I couldn't wait to get away."

His eyes narrowed again, and then he grinned like a man who'd just solved a difficult puzzle. "Rachel. You're Rachel Fleming. The town's been buzzing with the story that you're coming home."

It was too much to hope that the grapevine hadn't caught wind of her return. In a place the size of Canela, news spread quickly. Rachel's only hope was that the town didn't know all the details.

She looked at the man again, trying to place him. Though he sounded as though he knew her, she could swear she had never seen him before today. Surely she would have remembered a man with that lean physique and those chiseled features. He wasn't moviestar handsome, but he was definitely a man worth a second—or even a third—glance.

"It'll be good to be near my sister again," she said mildly. That was the only positive spin she could put on her return to Canela.

The two-way radio squawked. "Scott. Pick up if you're there." A man's voice crackled through the static.

The driver reached for the receiver. "Sanders here."

Rachel's eyes widened. "Sanders. You're Scott Sanders?"

*   *   *

"Aunt Rachel, wanna play catch with Doxy?" The four-year-old offered a rubber ball that had obviously spent most of its time in the dog's mouth.

Rachel shook her head. There were limits to an aunt's responsibility, and handling soggy pet toys was beyond them. "You go ahead, Danny. You're better at that than I am."

"I could teach you."

"Later, honey. Right now Aunt Rachel and I need to talk." The plump blonde tousled her son's dark brown hair, then pulled out one of the wrought iron chairs.

"Grown-ups. All you do is talk." The boy tossed the ball. "Go get it, Doxy."

"How is he?" Under his light tan, the boy was pale, and Rachel heard him breathing heavily, though he had run only a few yards.

"Holding his own." Becky's voice was so low that Rachel had to strain to hear her words; she knew her sister didn't want Danny to overhear them. "We have another appointment with the specialist next week. If everything's okay, he'll schedule surgery then."

Becky's eyes filled with tears as she looked at her son, now sitting on the grass, playing tug-of-war with his dog. Though to a casual observer, he appeared to be a normal four-year-old, Danny Barton's heart was anything but normal. He was born with a congenital defect, and had endured a series of operations which exhausted his parents' health plan and savings, leaving them with nothing but a heavily mortgaged house. A month ago the doctors had told Becky and Tim that the only thing that could save their son was a valve replacement, a horribly costly procedure. Even selling the house would not pay for the surgery. In desperation Becky and Tim had prayed for a miracle, until one day, a miracle happened.

"Rachel, Tim and I know how much we owe you. Someday. . . ."

"Don't thank me." Rachel's voice was fierce as she battled her own tears. "You'd have done the same. That's what sisters are for."

"Maybe so, but you're still the one who's making all the sacrifices. Giving up your job, leaving Dallas. . . ."

"Don't forget the biggie." Rachel took a long swallow of tea, trying to control her emotions. "I could have forgiven Grandma Laura the rest, but a husband? Leave it to that meddling old woman to mess with my life from the grave. Wasn't it enough that she tried to control everything I did for eighteen years?"

"I'm sure she had good intentions."

Rachel managed a wry smile. Her younger sister had always been the peacemaker in the family, while she had played the rebel. "You could call it that. I call it blackmail. Grandma knew I might turn down the money, but she was sure I'd never let you lose your share." Rachel gripped her glass. "And threatening to leave it to the Society for the Preservation of Squirrels!"

"Do you suppose there really is such a thing?"

"You bet there is." Unable to contain her anger, Rachel rose and started pacing the length of the patio. "That was the first thing I checked on. Then I had Art Langston look for every possible loophole. I was sure there was a way to break the will." She turned abruptly, her frustration evident. "There wasn't."

"At least you're sure. I guess that's one of the advantages of working for a law firm."

"It didn't help this time, did it? I'm still stuck with Grandma's meddling."

"Mom, look!" Danny laughed with glee as he held the ball over his head and the small dog leaped to reach it.

"You and Doxy are having fun, aren't you?" Rachel smiled. This was why she had come to Canela. Giving Danny a future was the only reason she'd endure the terms of her grandmother's will.

Though neither of her granddaughters had known it, Laura Fleming had been one of the wealthiest women in Canela, worth well over two million dollars. She had given Rachel and Rebecca a million dollars each, leaving the rest to charity. Unfortunately, the women's bequests had come with strings attached. In order for either Rachel or her sister to inherit any of the money, Rachel had to return to Canela and live in her grandmother's house for a year with her husband. A husband Rachel didn't have and didn't want.

"So, what are you going to do about a husband?" Becky asked. "Someone from the law firm?"

Rachel shook her head. "There's no one special in Dallas. Besides, I can't imagine any of the men I've dated giving up their jobs to move here."

"Canela's not so bad," her sister said with a fond glance at her yard. A row of pines shaded one side, while brightly colored flowers lined the fence. And in the middle of the yard, a small boy played with a brown dachshund. It might not be paradise, but for Becky Barton, it was close enough.

"What is this, the Canela Chamber of Commerce at work? You're the second person today who told me this is a good town."

"Who was the first?"

"Scott Sanders."

"So, what's Prickly Pear like these days?"

"Prickly Pear?" Scott looked up from his computer screen, his concentration broken by Luke's question. It was mid-afternoon, one of the quieter times at the gas station that Scott now owned, and he'd taken the opportunity to work on his income projections, confident that Luke could pump gas or handle any minor repairs.

"Rachel Fleming. You said that's her Mustang Jake's towing in."

"Ra—" Scott started to laugh. "I'd forgotten we used to call her that." He and Luke had been in Rachel's high school class, but even if they hadn't, in a town as small as Canela, all the teenagers knew each other. And though neither Scott nor Luke had ever dated Rachel, they had had their share of fantasies about the blue-eyed blonde who was the prettiest girl in the class. Unfortunately for them, she had eyes only for Brad Stewart.

"She's still prickly," Scott told his friend, "but she had definitely blossomed." Rachel looked different—softer somehow—although there was no denying the sharp edge of her tongue. Maybe it was her hair, a froth of golden curls that bounced on her shoulders. She had worn it short in school. And Scott would bet the down payment on his new underground storage tanks that she'd never owned a skirt that length when she lived with old Mrs. Fleming. Her grandmother had been notorious for keeping the two girls on a short leash. Scott frowned. Short leashes were something he knew all too well.

Luke settled into the small office's only comfortable chair, propping his feet on the edge of the desk. "I wonder if the rumor's true," he said as he leaned back. "Jessie claims she'll inherit big bucks if she stays here. Did Rachel say anything to you?"

"Gimme a break, Luke. Did you really expect her to start a conversation by telling me she's an heiress?" Scott glared at the screen, then saved the spreadsheet. "Tell you what. Why don't you ask her when she comes by to pick up your car."

"My car?" Luke's boots hit the floor with a thud.

"She needs wheels until we get the Mustang fixed. You can drive the Jimmy and give her your Pontiac."

Luke grinned. "I'd rather have the Jimmy, anyway."

"I kind of thought so. Now leave me alone, or I'll never get this blasted paperwork done."

An hour later, Scott was still typing formulas into the spreadsheet.

"I ordered the water pump," Luke said without preamble. "Two-day air."

Scott frowned. "Not soon enough."

"What do you mean? We always do two-day air."

At the sound of Luke's annoyance, Scott looked up. "What did you say?"

"Earth to Sanders. Earth to Sanders. What were you doing—working on the expansion plans?"

Scott nodded. "Yeah. That extra row of pumps

would make a big difference. If we had one more die-sel and two more high-test, we'd get the people who drive to Victoria mid-month when we usually run out."

"Let me guess. The problem is money."

"Isn't it always? There's got to be a way, Luke."

Scott switched off the computer and leaned back in his chair. Closing his eyes for an instant, he pictured Rachel Fleming sitting in his truck, telling him it wasn't her day. He grinned. If the rumors were true—and Canela rumors usually were—it just might be *his* day.

Chapter Two

A husband. She had thirty days—no, make that twenty-nine—to find one. Rachel swung her car into a parking spot in front of Shear Magic, then walked briskly into the beauty salon. With some luck, she would solve the problem today. For the first time since she had heard the terms of her grandmother's will, Rachel thought that fortune might be on her side. It had to be fate that he was one of the few single men in Canela and that he was home when she called him. Not only that, but he seemed eager to see her again. Yes, luck was improving.

Since she was a few minutes early for her appointment, and no one seemed to notice her entry, Rachel took a seat in the corner next to a tall silk plant.

"I heard she's back in town."

Though Rachel's grandmother had warned her of the dangers of eavesdropping, that was one of many admonitions which Rachel rarely heeded, particularly now, when eavesdropping might reveal just how much the townspeople knew of her circumstances. She

11

turned slightly to peer through the artificial plant leaves. Two women were seated in the salon, one having her nails buffed, the other waiting for her perm to set.

"Ellie Brown said she came for the money," the woman in curlers told the other. "It surely appears nothing else would have brought her back. Why, she didn't even have the decency to come for her grand-mother's funeral." The second woman's voice, though soft, left no doubt of her similar disapproval.

Rachel clenched her fists. She had been in a small town in western Montana when her grandmother had died, and there had been no way she could have re-turned to Canela in time for the funeral, because her grandmother had specified it must occur within twenty-four hours. Even in death, Laura Fleming had controlled events, preventing Rachel from being able to comfort her sister.

"What did you expect, Myrtle? She always was self-centered, even as a child."

"They say she hasn't changed at all." The woman named Myrtle raised her voice a few decibels as the beautician turned up the radio. "My mother always said leopards don't shed their spots."

"I don't know, Myrtle. Some people change. Look at the Sanders boy. The Marines surely made a man of him."

As the women's attention turned to Scott Sanders, Rachel began to relax. What they said wasn't pleasant, but—as Grandma always pointed out—the truth often isn't.

"Oh, Miss Fleming. I didn't hear you come in." The

receptionist welcomed her. "Sheila's ready for you now."

Her head held high with a confidence even a Marine might admire, Rachel walked into the salon. "Good morning, Mrs. Baker, Mrs. Henley." She greeted the two women with a warm smile, watching as an embarrassed flush colored their cheeks.

Once seated at the small table, she studied the selection of nail polishes. "This one will be perfect," she told Sheila. "Passionate pink." Let the gossips enjoy that tidbit!

She dressed with more care than usual for her luncheon meeting, choosing a navy suit that she'd bought for the law office and pairing it with a hot pink T-shirt to keep it from looking too business-like. This was, after all, a casual meeting of old friends . . . friends who might soon be much more.

Stay cool, she reminded herself as she drove to the Canela Motel. *Don't let him see how much this means.* And yet she couldn't help but smile a little ruefully. If this morning's episode at Shear Magic was any indication, everyone in Canela was aware of the most intimate details of her life.

He was sitting in a high-backed black vinyl chair, his back to the door, when she knocked.

"Come right on in, little lady," he said, spinning his chair around and getting to his feet. "What can I do for you?" His eyes moved from her golden curls to her navy-shod feet, lingering on the expanse of leg revealed by her skirt. Rachel had the unpleasant sensation that he was taking inventory of her parts as he might a selection of furniture for the motel he managed.

"Hello, Brad," she said in a voice that she hoped sounded both cool and friendly. "You haven't changed a bit." It was true. This man was still as handsome as ever.

"Rachel?" Brad's eyes widened, then narrowed as he took inventory again, this time more carefully. "You sure have changed," he declared, running his fingers through his hair in a gesture she remembered from high school. "Why, you're prettier than ever." He took a step closer, and ignoring Rachel's outstretched hand, pressed a quick kiss on her lips.

Rachel tasted mint mouthwash; she smelled lime aftershave; she felt nothing. How odd. When they were teenagers, she thought stealing kisses with Brad was the most wonderful experience imaginable. That was why he was first on her list—the only one on her list—of potential husbands. But today was different. Today, Brad's kiss evoked nothing, not even nostalgia. This wasn't turning out quite the way she had expected. But it would improve. It had to.

"I made a reservation at Maude's," Rachel said, referring to a restaurant a few miles outside of town.

"Good thinking, little lady. Maude's has lots of privacy." He winked at her as he ushered her out of the motel. "When Paula Sue and I were married, we used to go there for honeymoon afternoons, if you know what I mean. 'Course, Mary Jo used to prefer the good old Canela Motel. She always said we didn't have to waste time driving. Still, those dark booths in the back of Maude's are pretty good."

"Maude's must have changed." Rachel remembered it as a cheerful, tastefully decorated restaurant with excellent food, not as a dark place for lovers' trysts.

"You bet it has, little lady." Brad put his arm around Rachel's shoulders as they walked toward his car.

Rachel clenched her teeth, wondering how many more times Brad would call her "little lady", or ask if she knew what he meant. Surely he hadn't been like this in high school. It must have been his two failed marriages that changed him. But, whatever the cause, one thing was certain: Brad Stewart was not the answer to her problem.

"You know, Brad, maybe Maude's isn't such a good idea after all. Let's just have a burger at the Sonic for old times' sake."

"Whatever you say, little lady. I'm easy about things like that, if you know what I mean."

"I'm heading for the bank." Scott stuffed a few papers into a large manila envelope, then walked toward the gas station's front door.

"I hate to tell you this, boss," Luke drawled, "but you look like you're on the way to the electric chair. Sure you want to go through with this?"

Scott shook his head. "Wanting to and having to are two different things." As he drove into the center of town, Scott took a series of deep breaths at the thought of what was coming. He was going to break one of those unwritten rules that had formed the foundation of his life, and he hated the very thought of it. Still, as he had told Luke, there were some things a man had to do. Perhaps in this case the ends would justify the means.

The bank was filled with customers, people cashing checks on their lunch hour, businessmen making midday deposits, when Scott walked in. "Afternoon, Ms.

Hawley," he greeted the middle-aged woman who dispensed forms and cheerful advice. "If I could trouble you for a loan application. And then I'd like to see Ms. Hubble."

Three people stared as Scott moved to the counter and began to fill in the blanks. Half an hour later, he was ushered into the branch manager's small office.

"Your credit is good, Scott," Amy Hubble told him when she finished reviewing the forms. "There shouldn't be any problem getting the loan approved. Still," she said as she steepled her fingers and peered over her reading glasses, "I must admit I'm surprised. You're just about the last person in Canela I expected to be applying for a loan."

Though he knew what her response would be, Scott humored her by asking why.

"I knew your mother. Even when she knew how much you wanted to go to college, I couldn't convince her to take out a loan. She told me that the Sanders family didn't believe in debt."

Scott pointed to the application that bore his signature. "As you can see, Amy, I'm not my mother."

Before he had returned to the station, one third of Canela's population knew that Scott Sanders needed money . . . badly.

It was time. She had imposed on Becky and Tim long enough, trying to delay the inevitable. But, though they had welcomed her and told her that their sleeper sofa was hers for as long as she wanted to use it, she knew she had to move into the big old house on Prospect Street to fulfill the terms of Grandma Laura's will. And so, two days after her disastrous meeting with Brad Stewart, with twenty-six days remaining to find and marry a husband, Rachel unlocked the front door of the house that was to be her home for the next year.

Though she had expected dust or perhaps a musty smell, the house bore few signs of being unoccupied for six weeks. Rachel glanced into the formal parlor—Grandma could not abide the term 'living room'—and saw that the horsehair sofa, which predated the house itself, still stood next to the far wall. Dismissing the memories that that monstrously uncomfortable piece of furniture evoked, she grasped her suitcase handle and climbed the stairs. The door to her grandmother's room was closed, and as far as Rachel was concerned, it could remain closed for the entire year that she was a resident. Unless her husband wanted to sleep there.

Her husband. Rachel and Becky had spent hours trying to compile a list of eligible men after the Brad Steward fiasco. Yet, the list remained disappointingly short, for Rachel refused to consider Mr. Bingsley or any other widower old enough to be her father. The situation was bad enough without making it ludicrous. But excluding elderly gentlemen and Brad Stewart from the list left only two single men: Luke Johnson and Scott Sanders. Tonight she would flip a coin to see which one she would approach first.

At the sound of the doorbell, Rachel hurried back downstairs and looked through the peephole. There, standing on her front porch, was Scott Sanders. Two days earlier, she might have thought it was fate, that somehow he knew she'd been thinking of him, but her experience with Brad Stewart had taught her that if something seemed too good to be true, it probably was. In all likelihood, Scott had come to check on her car.

"It's running fine," she said, forestalling his question.

"Nice to see you, too, Rachel." A faint smile turned up the corners of Scott's mouth. "I'm glad to hear the car's fine, but that's not why I came."

For a second Rachel was disconcerted. Then she remembered the manners her grandmother had instilled. "Would you like to come in?"

Scott shook his head. "Is the gazebo still in the backyard?" When Rachel nodded, he continued. "Let's sit there."

She led the way, wondering why he had come and why he'd chosen the gazebo. Surely he had no way of knowing that it had been her favorite refuge as a child, a place to read, and dream, and share secrets with her sister.

"I've got a proposition for you," Scott said when they were seated in the fanciful building. The roof sheltered them from the midday sun, while the screened walls allowed the scent of freshly mown grass to perfume the air.

A proposition. Rachel arched her eyebrows.

"A business proposition." His tone was slightly ironic. He removed his Stetson, laying it on the bench next to him, and she saw that his hair was the same light brown it had been in his yearbook picture. But, although many men were wearing their hair longer now, Scott's remained short, perhaps a legacy of his years in the Marine Corps.

Scott swallowed, and Rachel had the sensation that he was somehow nervous. It seemed improbable, because Scott was far from being the shy, nerdy boy she remembered from high school; he was imbued with more than his share of self-confidence. That, more than the physical changes, was the reason she hadn't recognized him the other day.

"If the rumors are true," Scott said, "you need a husband."

"And if the rumors are true, you need a lot of money."

Scott smiled the confident I-own-the-world smile he seemed to wear as easily as his Stetson. "Let's deal with your problem first. Is it true?"

"The ever active Canela grapevine got it right." There was no reason to dissemble. "The full story is that my husband and I need to live in this house for a year in order for Becky and me to inherit."

"And Brad Stewart didn't make the grade?"

Rachel managed a wry smile. "The grapevine strikes again. I might have known that lunch at the Sonic was a mistake."

"From the stories I hear, his first two wives thought Brad Stewart was the mistake."

Rachel chuckled. "Brad might have a different perspective."

Dismissing Brad Stewart with a quick frown, Scott said, "It appears to me that you have a problem, and I might have a solution." He paused for a moment, turning to stare at her. Then the words tumbled out. "Rachel, I'd be honored if you'd become my bride."

It was not the way she had pictured it. As a child, when she had dreamed of a fairy tale marriage, she imagined a suitor kneeling before her. She assumed that proposals took place on dark, romantic nights with the scent of roses drifting around the happy couple—not at midday with freshly cut grass threatening to make her sneeze. As an adult—after Grandma's will had changed everything, that is—she had pictured herself sitting at a lawyer's table, presenting her plan to the man of her choice. Neither one had happened. Instead Scott Sanders was sitting in her gazebo, saying the words she had once thought her dream hero would utter.

"This is the business proposition you wanted to discuss?"

Scott nodded, his face still solemn. "Yes, Rachel. I'm willing to be your husband. The question is whether you're going to accept my proposal."

It appeared she didn't have to flip a coin to decide between Scott and Luke Johnson; rather than having to draft a husband, one had volunteered. Now all she had to do was accept him.

"We need to talk about the terms."

"Terms?"

"It's a business agreement, Scott. There are always terms and conditions."

"Ah, yes. I forgot that you used to work in a law office." His voice bore a hint of sarcasm.

"Surely you didn't expect me to swoon at your feet, telling you that I've loved you ever since high school and that I was counting the days until you asked for my hand."

Scott's mouth turned up in a crooked smile, almost as though he were trying not to grin. "A man wouldn't mind hearing words like that under the right circumstances. But if you told me that today, I'd know you were lying or trying to manipulate me. And one thing you should know right up front is that I don't take kindly to manipulation."

His words were so fierce that for a moment Rachel was speechless.

"Well, then, since we've agreed on that, let's talk about our marriage," she said at last. "You know that the term is a year."

"We can file for divorce at the end," Scott agreed. He settled back on the bench, crossing his arms, once again the picture of a confident cowboy.

"Actually, I was thinking of an annulment."

"An annulment?" Scott leaned forward, apparently surprised by her word. "How do you figure that? I may not be a lawyer, but I know there are specific requirements for getting an annulment."

Wanting to get this over quickly, Rachel nodded. The next, related, condition was going to be the most difficult to sell to Scott or any prospective husband. "There'll be no problem with an annulment," she said, "because this will be a marriage in name only."

Two furrows appeared between Scott's eyes. "Is that some legal term? Just what does it mean?"

"It means that we'll share a house but not a bed."

"You mean—"

"Exactly. We will not consummate the marriage."

He was silent for a long moment, his blue eyes fixed steadily on her face, as though he were trying to understand something.

"All right." Though his words were agreeable, his face remained grim.

Rachel let out a breath she hadn't been aware of holding. "Thanks, Scott. This means everything to my family."

"I know. Little Danny deserves a chance."

Rachel's eyes misted at the thought of her nephew. Then, reminding herself that there were still things to be settled with Scott, she continued, "One thing I learned at the law firm is that business arrangements are supposed to benefit both sides. It's obvious what Becky and I gain from this, but what about you? What can we give you?"

"You mean, since this won't be a normal marriage?"

Rachel blushed. "Well, yes. . . . "

"Let's be honest about this, Rachel. The rumor mill says you're going to inherit a million dollars. At the end of the year, I want half of it."

"Half a million dollars?" Somehow, although she heard that Scott needed money, she hadn't expected it to be so much.

"Those are the terms. Take them or leave them."

There was no choice, and Rachel knew it. Besides, Scott deserved some payment for his part in the arrangement.

"We've got a deal," she said, holding out her hand for the traditional shake. He ignored it. Instead, his eyes remained fixed on hers, and Rachel had the disconcerting thought that he was trying to see inside her, to fathom her innermost feelings. Uncomfortable, she dropped her gaze to the floor.

"Out of curiosity, what are you going to do with the money?" Rachel asked. When in doubt, change the subject. Put the other person on the defensive. "Your visit to the bank provoked almost as many phone calls as the return of the prodigal granddaughter. Only in your case, no one knew the details."

"Fair question," Scott agreed. "I'm going to expand

the station. A second row of pumps will make the difference between just breaking even and making a decent profit. And then there's the house." He paused, as if reluctant to continue. "I want to build a house for Justine."

"Justine?" Becky hadn't mentioned that Scott was involved with someone. Rachel had thought he and Luke were both unattached.

"She's a woman I met when I lived in Houston," Scott said smoothly. "We're planning to get married as soon as I'm settled here."

"I see." In fact, Rachel didn't understand. Scott's revelation raised new problems. "Won't Justine mind that you're marrying someone else?" Rachel knew that she would never agree to the man she loved living with another woman, even if it was only a marriage of convenience.

"Why would Justine mind?" Scott raised one brow and his blue eyes met hers with apparent guilelessness. "You said yourself that this is simply a business arrangement."

A business arrangement that was becoming stranger by the minute. "All right, Scott. We're agreed on this. The day that the lawyers write me a check for a million dollars, I'll give you half of it and we'll file for an annulment. But in the meantime, you can't see Justine. I don't want the lawyers to have any grounds for breaking the will. The Society for the Preservation of Squirrels is not going to get Danny's money!"

Scott was silent for a moment, his face set in the stern expression Rachel knew meant that he was thinking and didn't particularly like his thoughts. "I suppose that's reasonable," he agreed at last. "We can't jeopardize your inheritance. But that means we need to play this marriage game the right way. No one, and that includes your sister, can know that it's not a real marriage."

"We can trust Becky."

"No one." Scott's tone made it clear that there was no room for compromise on this particular condition. When Rachel nodded reluctantly, he continued. "In public we need to look like happy newlyweds. We won't give the lawyers any grounds for concern."

As unappealing as the stipulation was, Rachel had to admit that it made sense. There was too much at risk by not considering every aspect of the charade.

"There's one more thing."

The tone of Scott's voice made Rachel dread his next announcement. If it hadn't been childish, she might have plugged her ears.

"We're going to have a real wedding."

"But I thought we agreed—"

Scott shook his head. "We agreed on the terms of the *marriage*. The *wedding* is something else. We'll have the whole traditional hoopla. Long dress, tuxedos, church ceremony, reception at the country club, your nephew as the ring-bearer."

He sounded like a businessman ticking off the points of a proposed corporate merger. Why did that bother her? After all, she was the one who had insisted this was a business arrangement, nothing more. And yet . . . a little voice told her weddings weren't supposed to be like corporate mergers. Those childhood dreams of happily ever after seemed to have a habit of popping up at the wrong time.

"All right." Rachel nodded her head and rose to

leave the gazebo. She wouldn't make the mistake of offering her hand to him again. "I'll have Mr. Dundee draw up the agreement, giving you half the inheritance."

Scott rose, and Rachel was struck again by his bearing. Unlike many of the tall men she knew who tended to slouch, Scott stood as though he were proud of every inch of his height.

"There's one more thing. . . . "

She had no chance to anticipate his action. Moving so quickly, Scott drew her into his arms and lowered his lips to hers. His lips were surprisingly gentle as he pressed them to hers. Then as abruptly as he'd begun, Scott ended the kiss. He took a step backward, leaving Rachel oddly bereft, strangely cold now that his warmth was no longer next to her.

"We've got ourselves a deal," he said in a voice that was cool, calm, and one-hundred-percent businesslike.

That was what she wanted. Wasn't it?

Chapter Three

"Are you sure this is what you want to do?" The lawyer's voice held more than a hint of concern when Rachel explained why she was consulting him.

"Yes. I want Scott to have the money." Oddly enough, it was true. Half a million dollars was very little to pay for Danny's life, and without Scott, the boy would have no chance.

Harold Dundee nodded as he scribbled a few notes. "I'll have the agreement drafted tomorrow. Shall we say ten o'clock?"

Rachel slung her purse over her shoulder and walked toward the door.

"One more thing, young lady." She turned to face the attorney. "As your counselor, I'm not sure of the wisdom of giving the Sanders boy that much money, but as a friend, I can tell you he's a good man. Your grandmother would be proud to see you marrying him."

Biting back the reply that her grandmother's opinion no longer mattered, Rachel forced her mouth into a smile. "Good-bye, Mr. Dundee." What an awful thought, that Scott Sanders was a man her grandmother would have chosen for her! It was enough to make Rachel reconsider the agreement.

As she stepped into the hallway, her thoughts whirling, Rachel saw a familiar figure striding down the corridor. Scott! Was there no escaping the man? He moved quickly, as though he had no time to waste, and she wondered where he was going. The only tenants in the small office building were Canela's three attorneys. Why would Scott be visiting a lawyer? The image of a beautiful woman flashed across Rachel's mind. No, there was no reason Scott would consult a lawyer about Justine. It must be something for his station.

Dismissing the thought, Rachel headed home. She had a meal to prepare.

Four o'clock. Rachel checked her watch, mentally calculating the time she needed to finish dinner. The kitchen was redolent with the aroma of coq au vin, and the breadmaker was rocking and rolling during its second kneading cycle. All that was left to make was the dessert. While the cherry pie baked, she would set the table. China and crystal for Becky and Tim; plastic for Danny and Doxy. The dog, Becky had warned her, went almost everywhere Danny did.

Rachel was still smiling at the thought of the small dachshund curled on her nephew's bed when the doorbell rang.

"Dinner smells great." Scott sniffed appreciatively as he entered the house. He was wearing his signature jeans and chambray shirt, but today he carried a small paper bag. "I didn't know you could cook."

"Don't worry. I won't let you starve for a whole year."

"I wasn't worried," he countered. "I'm a mean hand with freezer cuisine and the microwave, but nothing I cook smells that good."

"I graduated to a slower cooker and breadmaker," she said, leading the way into the kitchen. As he sniffed again, she asked, "Want to stay for dinner and see if it tastes as good as it smells?" Though she had planned a quiet family dinner, tonight was as good a time as any for Scott to get to know Becky and Tim.

"That's a tempting thought, but I can't. I just stopped by to bring you this." Scott reached into the paper bag and drew out a square velvet box that could hold only one thing.

For a second Rachel merely stared. Then she clenched her hands. "I can't accept that." Rings were for real engagements, not charades. Though his previous conditions had made sense, Scott was going too far if he thought she was going to wear his ring.

"You haven't even looked at it," Scott said, his voice gruff with what sounded like anger.

"It doesn't matter. I won't wear a ring."

"I thought we had agreed that this was going to look like a real marriage." This time there was no mistaking the anger in his voice.

"Well, yes, but . . . I didn't think. . . ."

"That's exactly the problem, Rachel. You're so caught up with yourself that you never think about other people. Didn't it occur to you that I might not want to look like a gigolo?"

Rachel flinched as though he'd struck her. It was true. She'd been so concerned about getting the money for Danny's operation that she hadn't considered how the townspeople might view Scott's part in the marriage.

"But you *are* marrying me for the money," she said in her own defense.

"That's between you and me. No one else is supposed to know that."

"Except Mr. Dundee. The lawyer," she added, when Scott looked at her blankly.

"Right. Now, why don't you try this on." He snapped the box open and handed it to Rachel.

For a moment she was silent, staring at the most magnificent ring she had ever seen. A diamond flanked by twin sapphire baguettes was set in a wide gold band that somehow looked both modern and traditional. It was more than beautiful; it was the ring of her dreams. From childhood on she had wanted sapphires in her engagement ring. Then, when she and her friends had grown old enough to visit Canela's jewelry store, she had discovered that wide bands flattered her fingers. Now Scott Sanders was offering her the perfect ring. How had he known? Rachel shook her head. It was pure coincidence that Scott had chosen this ring; that's all.

Scott lifted the ring out of the box and handed it to her.

"It's beautiful," she said softly as she slid it onto her finger.

"We aim to please." Scott stared at her for a long moment, and Rachel wondered if he was going to kiss her as he had when they'd made their agreement. It wasn't that she wanted him to, of course. It was simply that Scott seemed to put a lot of stock in tradition, and this *was* a traditional time for a kiss. But Scott made no move toward her. Instead he stuffed his hands into his jeans pockets and turned toward the door. "Gotta go. I'll be back on Monday."

"You're going away for the weekend?" Though they had made no plans, it was only a week before the wedding, and Rachel had assumed he would stay in Canela.

Scott nodded. "I'm going to Houston."

"Houston, as in Justine?"

"There's only one Houston that I know of." Scott moved toward the door as though he couldn't wait to get there.

"But I thought we agreed that you wouldn't see her."

"After the wedding, Rachel. Until then, I'm a free man."

And she was a free woman. The problem was, tonight that freedom brought her no joy.

"You're wearing a ring!" Becky had taken only two steps into the house when she spotted the diamond on Rachel's left hand. "Let me see it. Oh, Tim, look at the ring Scott gave Rachel."

"Nice."

"Nice?" Becky chided her husband. "It's fabulous."

When Tim and Danny had gone into the backyard to play catch with Doxy while Rachel finished dinner, Becky settled back in one of the kitchen chairs. "That is one gorgeous rock you've got, sister dear," she said. "I'll bet that's why Scott needed a loan. Everyone knows he's been plowing all the profits back into the station."

"Maybe," Rachel lied. She knew that Scott no longer needed a loan now that he had the promise of half her inheritance, but she couldn't tell Becky. When the year was over, she promised herself she would share the whole story with her sister. In the meantime, she would abide by her agreement with Scott.

"Did you find a gown?" Becky asked when they'd finished dinner and Tim had retired to the sun porch.

Rachel shook her head. She had visited Canela's sole bridal shop and had found nothing that suited her, and Susie Garland, the town's seamstress who might have made a dress for her, was vacationing in Alaska.

"I'll have to go to Dallas tomorrow," she said. Though she had planned to shop in Houston, there was no force on earth that would get her to travel in that direction now that she knew Scott and Justine would be there.

"I'd offer you my gown," Becky said, "but it won't fit." Becky was three inches shorter than her sister, and though they weighed the same, the pounds were distributed differently. "I've got an idea. Why don't we look in the attic? I'll bet Grandma's gown is there. It would probably fit you."

"Not on your life! I'd rather go naked than wear her dress."

"Now, that would give Canela something to talk about, wouldn't it?" Becky laughed and grabbed her sister's hand. "Let's try the attic."

It was surprising what treasures the third floor held. There were trunks of men's garments, some of which Rachel suspected were a hundred years old, and boxes of old books. But the real treasure store was the cedar closet with its cache of formal gowns.

As Becky had predicted, their grandmother's wedding dress had been carefully preserved. Though Rachel ignored it, her hand lingered on a gown of silk and gossamer lace that had obviously belonged to a woman of an earlier generation. At Becky's urging, she tried on the dress and found that, with only a few simple alterations, it would fit her. Becky's veil and her own white shoes would complete the costume.

The pieces were all coming together, she thought, as she dusted the sideboard in the dining room the next morning. In one week, she would be married, and two days after that, Mr. Dundee would release a portion of Becky's inheritance. Although Grandma's will had stipulated that the women would receive the bulk of the estate only at the end of the one-year term, there had been a clause which allowed judicious early dispersal for medical emergencies. Grandma Laura seemed to have known just how much Becky would need the money.

What Rachel couldn't understand was why their grandmother had risked her only great-grandchild's life. She couldn't have been one hundred percent certain that Rachel would agree to the terms of the will. And yet, knowing just how determined Laura Fleming had been, Rachel suspected she hadn't even considered that Rachel might refuse. Grandma had thought that all she had to do was command, and everyone would obey. They usually did.

Rachel plugged in the vacuum cleaner, trying not to think of the many Saturdays she and Becky had spent dusting and vacuuming. A woman with Laura Fleming's money could have afforded to have a cleaning service. Instead, she had insisted that her granddaughters keep the house not just clean but immaculate.

The Fleming house had been a far cry from Lydia Sanders' cottage. The one time Rachel had gone there to deliver a homework assignment for Scott, she'd been appalled. Every flat surface had been covered with books and magazines thrown in haphazard piles, and a thick layer of dust had coated all but a few of the piles. Rachel had wrinkled her nose, trying not to sneeze. Mrs. Sanders, it appeared, did not share her grandmother's passion for cleanliness.

She also did not share Mrs. Fleming's disdain for expressions of affection. While Rachel could not remember her grandmother ever hugging her, Scott's mother walked to school with him each morning, kissing him good-bye. The other children had mocked Scott mercilessly, calling him a Mama's boy. No wonder he'd been shy and nerdy.

But, oh, he had changed! The chubby boy who'd never spoken in class—who had been Luke Johnson's shadow—had become a lean, muscled man who cast his own shadow. Perhaps it was irony, perhaps poetic justice, that now Luke worked for Scott.

Who would have thought that Brad Stewart, the high school hunk, would turn into a matrimonial disaster and that Scott, having waited so long to marry, would find himself in his current situation: in love with one woman, engaged to another? It was definitely a case of truth being stranger than fiction.

He had less than forty-eight hours to finish his plans, explain as much as he could under the circumstances, and return to Canela. It did not promise to be the most pleasant weekend of Scott Sanders' life.

When he reached the outskirts of Houston, Scott stopped at a florist's shop. He could have bought the flowers in Canela, but the grapevine would have quickly realized that the flowers weren't for Rachel, and that would have raised unwanted speculation. It was better this way.

As he had so many times before, he parked the car in front, opened the wrought iron gate and walked the few steps to where he knew she would be waiting. Taking a deep breath, he began to speak. "I won't be coming here for the next year . . . maybe longer."

There was no answer, but he hadn't expected any. The scent of the white lilies that she had always loved filled the air. "You see, I'm getting married. I never thought I'd be saying this, but I'm marrying Rachel Fleming."

He unwrapped the cellophane from the flowers, folding it into a square as carefully as if it were a flag. "I don't expect you to understand or approve. It's too late for that." He closed his eyes for a second, as though to block out his surroundings. "This is something I have to do. And, yes, I want to. There's a little boy's life at stake. But, no matter what happens, I'll always love you."

Scott bent down and placed the lilies on his mother's grave.

It was beautiful and sunny, the kind of day any bride would want. If this had been a real wedding, the weather was exactly what Rachel would have ordered. But it wasn't a real wedding; it was a charade, and the light breeze, moderate temperatures, and low humidity seemed to mock her.

"Danny's so excited," Becky said as she pinned Rachel's veil into place. "It was all Tim and I could do to convince him he couldn't bring Doxy with him."

"That would certainly have made this a wedding to remember." Rachel considered the picture of her ring-bearer being trailed by his dachshund. What would Scott have thought of that bridal procession?

"Sally Mae Jensen is going to be furious, but I'd say you're giving Canela its wedding of the year. Everyone's talking about what a perfect couple you and Scott are."

A perfect couple. Rachel could have found other words to describe them.

"Tell me, Rachel," Becky continued, "are you happy? I know you didn't want to get married, and you're doing this for Danny, but we've never really talked about how you feel about Scott."

Rachel looked at her reflection in the long mirror. With her white gown and veil, she looked like a bride, and she had promised Scott that she would act like one. "You wouldn't believe me if I told you I was madly in love with Scott," she said slowly, "and I'm not. But we understand each other. I'd say that's a pretty good foundation for any marriage, wouldn't you?"

As she walked down the church aisle, holding Tim's arm and hearing the traditional wedding march, she wasn't so sure. How could she stand before the minister and the people of Canela and promise to love and cherish this man she hardly knew? For a moment she was tempted to turn and run. Then she looked at the small figure who walked a few paces ahead of her. For Danny she could do almost anything.

She raised her eyes, and when they met Scott's, he smiled. Rachel's step faltered. Who would have dreamt that a man could look like that? It wasn't just the tuxedo that fit him as well as his jeans and boots; clothes were only part of the picture. When he looked at her, Scott smiled as if she were the only person in the world, the woman he had been waiting for all his life.

Rachel's heart began to pound, and she could feel her face begin to flush. Then she heard the people in the next pew murmuring, and reality returned. It was all an act. Scott was doing what he had promised, giving her a wedding no lawyer could contest, with his Academy Award performance of a happy groom.

Though she must have made the correct responses during the ceremony, Rachel's only memories of the brief service were of Scott's face as she approached him and of his reaction when the minister declared that he could kiss the bride.

At the minister's signal, he took a step forward, wrapped his arms around her and lowered his lips to hers. It was a moment of pure magic, the sensation of his mouth on hers, his hands caressing her back.

"Aunt Rachel, is it time to cut the cake?"

As the congregation began to laugh, Scott's lips relinquished hers. But he held her hand as they walked from the church, and for the rest of the afternoon, he remained by her side.

"Is it true that you loved Rachel when you were in school together?" one of the guests asked.

Scott put his arm around Rachel's shoulders, drawing her closer to him and pressing a kiss on the top of her head. "Every male in our class had a crush on Rachel," he said with a fond smile. "But I'm the lucky guy she agreed to marry."

"You waited quite a while, though." The guest was as persistent as an investigative reporter.

"I'd say she's worth the wait. Wouldn't you?"

The words were sweetly romantic, exactly what someone might expect from a besotted bridegroom. Only Rachel and her groom knew that they were meaningless, designed to dispel rumors and convince skeptical attorneys.

If the ceremony had seemed brief, the reception was endless. Rachel's face ached from keeping a smile fixed on it, and if one more woman asked to see her ring, she thought she would scream. She didn't know what was worse, the compliments on her engagement ring or the ribald comments about the wedding night to come. If the gossips knew the truth about the wedding night and what wasn't going to happen, the Canela phone lines would be smoking.

At last Scott proposed one final toast, announcing that the party could continue, but he and his bride were going home. Rachel's relief was so great that she almost sighed until she remembered that a happy bride would giggle with pleasure, not sigh with relief.

Her relief was premature. Not only did a group of guests accompany them to the front of the country club, but there would be no silent departures, for Rachel's Mustang had been festooned with paper flowers, balloons, streamers, and a large complement of tin cans.

"You wanted a real wedding," she muttered as Scott

started the engine and they pulled away to the accompaniment of clanking cans.

"What's wrong, Rachel? Isn't this your idea of music?"

His voice was cool, the impersonal tone he normally used when they were alone. This was the Scott she knew, not the one who'd spoken in a warm, intimate voice all afternoon. Who would ever have thought that he would be such a good actor? Not once had he stepped out of character. It appeared Scott Sanders was wasting his talents pumping gas and repairing cars in east Texas when he could become the next Hollywood sensation.

They headed back to the house on Prospect Street. Though she had been unable to refuse the engagement ring, Rachel had insisted that there would be no honeymoon. Officially, they had told people that they were waiting until after Danny's surgery. It was a plausible story. Once the surgery was successful, Rachel would invent another reason for a delay.

Scott pulled the car into the garage, then took Rachel's hand as they walked toward the house. When she moved toward the back door, he shook his head and led the way to the big front porch.

"What . . . ?"

Instead of answering, Scott swept her into his arms. With her long gown trailing and her head cradled so close to his chest that she could hear the steady beat of his heart, he carried her over the threshold and into the hallway. Rachel closed her eyes. It was indulgent, no doubt about it, but for a moment longer she pretended this was a real wedding, not a pretense designed to satisfy the letter of her grandmother's will.

As Scott turned to the right, Rachel opened her eyes, then gasped. It was her house, the one where she had been raised, the one she couldn't wait to escape. And yet it wasn't the same at all. The front parlor where Scott had brought her had been transformed into a romantic bower. Masses of roses, daisies, and lilacs filled the room with their fragrances, while the strains of soft music transported her to another era. Even the horsehair sofa had been disguised, hidden under a silken cover whose jeweled tones complemented the Persian carpet.

"Welcome home, Mrs. Sanders." Scott released her so that she could once again stand. Though her feet were on solid ground, her legs felt as though they were made of rubber. Scott held her close to him, and the heat that radiated from him threatened to melt even her strongest resolve. But it was his smile that was her undoing. His eyes were warm with affection, leaving Rachel no doubt that he was going to kiss her again. And this time there would be no Danny to interrupt him.

Scott stared at her for a moment longer, his eyes asking a question she could not answer. Then he lowered his arms and walked briskly toward the fireplace. Uncorking a bottle of champagne, he filled two flutes and handed one to Rachel.

"You were a beautiful bride," he said, his voice cool and businesslike as he touched the rim of his glass to hers. "The lawyers should have no doubts about this wedding."

Rachel managed a smile, remembering Danny and the reason for the wedding. That was safe ground, talking about the lawyers, but as she looked around,

Rachel felt as though she were on quicksand. She understood the smiles, the kisses, the flowery words, everything Scott had done up to and including carrying her over the threshold. He was an actor, performing for an audience, just as she had been an actress when she smiled and pretended that this was a fairy tale wedding with Prince Charming claiming his bride after years of separation. That all made sense. It was part of their agreement. But nothing explained why he had turned her house into a dream setting.

"I don't understand," she said, gesturing to the room. "No one can see us now."

Scott was silent for a moment, his face somber. He finished his champagne and placed the flute on the mantel before he spoke. "It's a dress rehearsal," he said at last. "For Justine."

Chapter Four

Guilt. It was not an emotion he experienced regularly. Oh, his mother had tried to make him feel guilty when he wanted to join extra curricular activities in high school, or when he preferred to spend Saturday afternoons playing ball with Luke instead of listening to the opera with her. Half the time she had succeeded. Then he had joined the Marines, where he learned to make his own decisions, to trust in himself, and not to feel guilty when he didn't accede to others' unreasonable demands. Guilt had disappeared from his daily life, which made it all the more uncomfortable this morning. Particularly because he knew he was wrong. He *was* guilty.

Scott frowned as he looked around the kitchen. With its eastern exposure and lemon-yellow walls, it was a cheerful room. Today that cheerfulness seemed to mock him, reminding him he had no reason to be happy. He had caused Rachel pain that she didn't deserve. She had the highest of motives for their marriage. If his weren't as noble, that was still no reason for hurting her. And there was no doubt that his reference to Justine had caused her pain. He would be more careful in the future. In the meantime. . . .

Scott pulled the English muffins from the toaster oven, slipped a poached egg on each, then drizzled hollandaise sauce over them. He grimaced as he poured two glasses of orange juice and placed them on the large silver tray. It seemed that many things in his life were missing a critical ingredient, starting with the eggs Benedict and ending with his marriage. Who ever heard of eggs Benedict without Canadian bacon or a marriage with separate bedrooms? Though a trip to the supermarket could solve the first problem, Scott saw no easy cure for the second. If the past twenty-four hours were any indication, it was going to be a long year.

"What are you doing here?" Rachel demanded as he entered her room. She had wakened at the sound of his footsteps on the hardwood floor, brushing her hair from her face and sliding her back up against the headboard.

Scott took a deep breath. If anything, she was even more beautiful than she'd been the day before. Rachel wore no makeup, her hair was tousled, and she frowned at him, yet she was still an enchanting sight. What red-blooded male wouldn't want to accept the challenge of kissing that frown into a smile, of running his fingers through those wayward curls, of discovering whether her cheeks were as soft as the petals of the yellow rose he had placed next to her breakfast?

Swallowing deeply, Scott set the tray on one of the bedside tables. "I should think it's fairly obvious," he said as he turned back to her. "I've brought us break-fast."

"Us?" How could one word hold so much contempt?

"One, two." He gestured toward the cups, plates and glasses. "I think you'll find there are two of everything."

Rachel's eyebrows rose as she pulled the sheets higher until nothing more than her neck and shoulders was exposed. "There's only one person who's going to eat in this room," she announced.

Which was probably a good thing, considering the direction Scott's thoughts were headed. "I hadn't realized just how appropriate your nickname was," he said in an attempt to think about something, anything other than the sexy creature in that bed.

"What nickname?" she demanded. "I don't have one."

"Shows what you know." Scott stared at her for a moment, willing his eyes to move no lower than her face. "In school we all used to call you 'Prickly Pear.'"

"Prickly Pear?" Her eyes widened as she considered the sobriquet, and he could tell that she was puzzled. It was little wonder. This room was so soft and feminine with its lace curtains and the canopied bed that it was difficult to think about anything as sharp and wild as a cactus.

"You know, Prickly Pear like the cactus. You used those long thorns to keep everyone away from you." Scott picked up the coffeepot and poured her a cup, ignoring the glare she gave him. "Of course, I always figured you were just doing what the cactus does and protecting a sweet heart. Was I right?"

"That's one thing you're never going to find out." Her words were fierce, but as she looked at the yellow rose he had so carefully placed on the tray, Scott saw her expression soften. "Thanks for the breakfast," she said at last. She sniffed the coffee longingly, and Scott realized she wanted to reach for it but was uncomfortable in his presence.

"I can take a hint," he said. "I'll leave you alone, but be ready at two. Casual clothes and bring a jacket." He started toward the door.

"Where are we going?"

"It's a surprise."

"What if I don't want to go?"

"Tough." Scott took a step back into the room. "This is all part of the plan. You remember it, don't you, Rachel—the convince-the-lawyers plan?"

"We're supposed to be on our honeymoon," she protested, color rising to her cheeks.

"Exactly. No one would expect us to leave the house this morning, but even honeymooners have to come up for air."

She had to admit that it was a perfect day, at least as far as the weather was concerned. Rachel couldn't fault the blue skies and low humidity. It was only the conditions inside the house that disturbed her equilibrium more than a thunderstorm. She couldn't even blame Scott. He seemed to be trying to make the day a pleasant one. And, though she hated to admit it, he was probably right that they ought to make some kind of public appearance.

They took her Mustang, minus the cans. Rachel would have removed the flowers and streamers, not to mention the huge "Just Married" sign, but once again Scott was adamant. He loaded a picnic basket and blanket into the small trunk, then gallantly helped Rachel into the passenger's seat before sliding behind the wheel. Rachel suppressed a smile at the sight of Scott folding his six-foot frame into the low seat. Though they had driven together before, she had never noticed how he filled the car.

"Where are we going?" Rachel asked when they crossed the town line.

Scott flashed her a mocking grin. "What part of 'surprise' don't you understand?"

As though forestalling her questions, he reached into the seat pocket and slid a tape into the dash. Though Rachel expected something soft and romantic like the music he had provided the night before, the car was soon filled with hit songs from their graduation parties. Oh, the memories! Closing her eyes, Rachel could picture herself in cap and gown, gripping her diploma and grinning—not from the joy of finishing high school but from the knowledge that in mere hours she would be on her way to Dallas. Big D, city lights, freedom. Now here she was, thirteen years later, back in Canela, married under circumstances that she could never have imagined. And the man who sat next to her, who had shared those high school years with her, was just as much of an enigma now as he had been then. Scott Sanders. Her classmate. Her husband. The world had definitely turned upside down.

As Scott swung the car onto a dirt road, Rachel opened her eyes. "River Road?" Scott was heading toward Canela High's favorite parking spot, a bend in the river where live oaks grew close to the water, a spot whose popularity owed much to the fact that it was forbidden by virtually every parent. And, though Rachel had defied many of her grandmother's edicts, that was one she had never dared to flout. "I thought this was a nighttime spot," she said as Scott parked the car. During the warmer months, swimming had vied in popularity with parking.

Scott laughed as he opened her door and helped her out, holding her hand an instant or two longer than absolutely necessary. Today for the first time, he wore shorts rather than long pants, and she couldn't help noticing how firmly muscled his legs and thighs were. True to what the women in the beauty shop said, the Marines had made a man out of a gangling, awkward teenage Scott. "You can do all the swimming you want," she declared, determined that she would not blush at the thought of shedding clothes. "I, for one, have no intention of getting wet."

Scott shrugged. "Tempting as the thought is, I figured we'd settle for a picnic." He spread a blanket under one of the largest trees, then drew a thermos and two glasses from the basket. "Lemonde, anyone?"

Her back propped against the tree, Rachel sipped her drink and watched the river flowing slowly by them. A few bees buzzed, and she heard a bird calling to its mate, but it appeared that most of the world was as content with silence as she and Scott were. It was odd to realize she was spending her first visit ever to River Road with her husband, and that they were doing nothing more than enjoying the beautiful setting.

How many other Canela High students could make that claim?

"Why did you join the Marines?" she asked at length.

Scott gave her a long appraising look, as if he were trying to guess why she had asked the question. "The usual reasons, I suppose. I wanted to see the world, get an education, get away from here."

Those were reasons Rachel could understand. "But you came back." That was the part she didn't fathom. "Why'd you do that? You don't have any family left here."

"It'll probably sound odd to you, but Canela's home."

"Not for me." The words tumbled out, seemingly without volition. "Home" and "Canela" were two words she preferred to keep well-separated.

Scott raised an eyebrow. "Then where is home for you, Rachel? Dallas?"

Her response should have been immediate agreement. Instead, Rachel found herself saying slowly, "I suppose so."

His glass empty, Scott stretched out on the blanket, crossing his arms behind his head. If Rachel had been an artist, she would have painted him with the caption, "Man at Rest." Unlike most of the people she knew, Scott seemed content with silence and repose. He appeared to have no need to fill every moment with empty conversation, but when he did ask a question, it was clear he expected an answer.

"Did you like working for lawyers?" he asked. Though his eyes were half-closed, she sensed that he was watching her carefully, the way he had when he'd asked about home.

She should have been able to respond affirmatively. The fact that she found herself hesitating irritated Rachel. "What is this?" she demanded. "An interrogation?"

Scott opened his eyes and stared at her, his expression mildly reproachful. "I thought we were having a conversation," he said. "Ever hear that term? I figured that if we were going to be living together, we ought to get to know each other."

"We're not living together!"

"Ah, Rachel." Scott chuckled softly. "You haven't lost your prickliness."

As the afternoon sun began to set, Scott cleared away the remains of their picnic, then extended a hand to Rachel. "Come on. We don't want to be late."

"For what?" Despite their few minutes of disagreement, it had been an unusually enjoyable afternoon, and Rachel was reluctant to see it end.

"What would you say if I told you we were going to a drive-in movie?"

"Absolutely, positively no!"

Scott laughed. "You're right. Honeymooners wouldn't go to a drive-in. They're past that stage."

He drove a few miles to the east, then turned down a small country road. It was only when she saw the sign "Up, Up and Away" that Rachel knew where they were heading.

"Hot air balloons."

"Ever been in one?" Scott asked, carefully negotiating the rutted road.

"No." She wasn't going to tell Scott that a balloon

ride had been one of her dreams but that her salary didn't extend to such extravagances.

"Me neither." For a second she thought he was going to say something else, but Scott remained silent until he parked the car.

"Just in time," Hans, the balloonist, said, pointing toward the brightly colored fabric that lay on the ground. He asked for their help in spreading out the balloon, then positioning the fans to inflate it. Rachel darted from side to side, fascinated by the sight of the expanding balloon, while Scott helped Hans wheel a wicker basket from the garage. Once the propane tanks were attached, Hans gestured to Rachel and Scott and another couple to climb into the basket.

"Are you honeymooners?" the other woman asked Rachel.

As if in response, Scott slid his arm around Rachel's shoulders, drawing her closer to him.

"I thought so." The woman told Rachel that she and her husband were celebrating their silver anniversary.

Hans adjusted the propane torch once more, then slowly the balloon began to rise.

As the staff on the ground waved, Rachel smiled so much that her cheeks ached. "Oh, Scott." She leaned back into the circle of his arms, smiling with pleasure as the farm buildings grew smaller. It was magic, pure magic, drifting with the wind currents, climbing when Hans fired the propane tanks, then gliding silently, watching the scenery unfold beneath them. "This is wonderful." It was different, far more intimate than being in a plane. Even though Hans and the other couple shared the basket, Rachel felt as if she and Scott were in their own private world. "It's even better than I dreamed," she said softly.

Scott drew her closer and pressed a kiss on the top of her head. Of course it was an illusion, as everything else about the marriage was, but for a moment Rachel felt cherished and protected, and that was even more magical than the balloon flight itself.

All too soon it was over. With a soft thump Hans landed the balloon in another farmer's field, then reached out to secure the basket. As soon as the balloon was rolled and stuffed into its bag, the chase crew had sparkling cider ready.

Rachel and Scott touched their glasses to the other couple's, then sipped. When Rachel swallowed, Scott took the glass from her and laid it carefully on the ground. As if in slow motion, he drew her once more into his arms, then placing his hands on either side of her face, he lowered his lips to hers. When he broke away, she was left feeling bereft.

They were silent once more as they drove back to Canela, but this silence was far different from the one at the river. That had been comfortable, companionable. This one was awkward. She smelled the faint lime from his aftershave; she heard his breathing. And she berated herself every mile of the way back.

Why, oh, why, did she respond to him? She could have remained impassive in his arms, letting him kiss her. But no, not Rachel. She returned his kiss with every bit of the intensity he gave her.

She could rationalize it, saying it was good that they didn't hate each other. After all, they had to share a house for a year. But there was a big difference—an enormous difference—between being friendly and sharing passionate embraces. Honeymooners kissed the way they had, but business associates—which is what they were—did not engage in romantic kisses.

And then there was Justine. How on earth could she have let herself behave that way with another woman's man? Had she no shame, no common sense? Rachel knew why Scott had kissed her, but why had she responded?

"I assume that today was another dress rehearsal," she said as they neared Canela. "The picnic and balloon ride were practice for Justine."

The lights of an oncoming car played on Scott's face, revealing his smile. "Oh, no," he said, obviously amused by her question. "Justine isn't much for outdoor activities."

"Then why did you plan all this?"

"I thought that was obvious. Today was for you." Scott paused, as if waiting for Rachel's response. When she said nothing, he continued. "And for the attorneys."

Sleep eluded her. She had tried everything she knew, from reading a book to watching TV to counting cattle, which Texans preferred to sheep. Nothing worked. Her brain seemed to be in overdrive, replaying the events of the day, preventing her from sleeping. Finally she slipped on her robe and headed for the kitchen. Perhaps her grandmother's cure of warm milk and graham crackers would prove effective in battling insomnia.

Rachel descended the stairs, wincing as they creaked. When she entered the main hall, she heard Scott's voice. Surprised that he was still awake and appeared to have a visitor, she walked toward the small den.

Scott's voice was low and intimate, a tone she'd never heard. "I wish I could be with you every minute of every day," she heard him say. "If I were, I could show you just how much I love you."

Once more ignoring her grandmother's admonitions about eavesdropping on what was obviously a private conversation, Rachel moved closer to the doorway.

"When I think about how sweet your lips taste. . . . "

Rachel felt warmth rise to her cheeks as she remembered just how sweet Scott's mouth had been. And now it appeared he was planning to savor someone else's lips under her very roof. The audacity of the man!

She stormed into the den, her hands clenched in anger, demanding who the woman was. But the room was empty except for Scott, who sat in the deep wing chair, his head tipped so he could cradle the phone against his shoulder.

Scott looked up, raising his brows as if surprised to see Rachel. "I'll call you back, darling," he said into the phone, his words a caress. As he carefully replaced the receiver, he rose to his feet and towered over Rachel, his annoyance evident in his frown.

"Who was that?" He mimicked her question. "That was Justine. Not that it's any of your business."

Justine. Of course. The woman he loved. The woman he wanted to marry.

"It *is* my business," Rachel insisted, feeling anger and something else—something she didn't want to identify—shoot through her. "You agreed you wouldn't see Justine while we were married."

"That's true." Scott nodded. "I gave you my word, and I always keep it." Though his mien was serious, his blue eyes sparkled with something that looked strangely like amusement. "You'll notice I didn't *see* Justine."

Darn it all. He was right.

Chapter Five

"I didn't expect you here this early." Luke leaned against the doorframe, coffee mug in hand, a puzzled expression on his face.

"What do you mean?" Scott pretended he didn't understand Luke's comment. Though he had shared many confidences with Luke over the years there were some things—most notably the circumstances of his marriage—that Luke had no business knowing. "I'm usually here before you," he pointed out.

"But you're a honeymooner."

"Yeah?" Scott drained his coffee, then pushed back his chair. Considering the amount of sleep he hadn't gotten last night, he would need a constant infusion of caffeine to keep him functioning today. And Luke would grin each time he poured a cup, thinking he knew the reason for Scott's fatigue. He wouldn't be that far wrong, either. The last two sleepless nights had one—and only one—cause: Rachel.

"I may be a honeymooner, as you put it," Scott said when he'd taken a long slug of the strong black brew, "but I haven't forgotten what Mondays are like here. You'd be hard-pressed to handle the customers alone."

As if on cue, two cars pulled up to the pumps, a truck parked in front of the garage doors, and the phone began to ring. It was an hour later when Luke pushed open the door to the closet Scott called an office.

"That was quite some wedding you and Rachel had." Luke had switched from coffee to soda as his source of caffeine, Scott heard the distinctive sound of the pull tab. He kept his eyes focused on his paperwork, unwilling to enter into a discussion of his marriage. But the subtlety appeared to be lost on Luke. "Looking at you two could almost make a man believe in happy endings," Luke drawled. "If he was so inclined, that is."

Scott's head jerked up in surprise. Luke's voice held a note he hadn't heard in a long, long time. "It's been ten years," Scott said, his own voice as neutral as he could make it. "Isn't it about time you thought about settling down?"

It was the wrong question. The black look on Luke's face told him his friend wasn't ready for that particular line of questioning. "Just because you're caught in the commitment trap doesn't mean it's gonna snare me, too." Luke gripped the can so tightly it began to crumple. "And don't tell me stories about getting back on a horse after you've been thrown. I've heard them all a hundred times."

"Hey, man—"

"Don't 'hey man' me. I lived through hell once, and that's enough for me."

Scott grimaced, sorrier than he could ever say that

he'd raised the specters of his friend's past. Unlike Scott, Luke had married soon after high school, and had what everyone believed to be the perfect marriage. But perfection had ended one short year later when Luke's wife and baby daughter had died from complications of childbirth. In the space of a few hours, Luke had gone from a happily married man and proudly expectant father to a man who shunned every form of commitment. He had sold his house, given away his dog, and now lived in a small apartment with not so much as a potted plant for company.

And yet he seemed oddly content in his solitary lifestyle, insisting that he had everything he needed or wanted. Though Scott doubted the latter, he valued Luke's friendship too much to challenge him openly. He would not mention marriage again.

But Luke had no such compunctions. They were sitting in the office, styrofoam containers of food opened on the desk as they took a late lunch break. Mondays were always busy, but this one had been more hectic than usual—the direct result, Luke claimed, of Scott's wedding. According to Luke, everyone in Canela wanted to see the new bridegroom.

"Looks like you've developed a taste for cactus," Luke said as he swallowed a bite of the coleslaw that accompanied their barbecued chicken. "I never saw a man as infatuated as you were with Prickly Pear. To tell you the truth, I wouldn't have believed it if I hadn't been there myself."

Scott managed a smile. Luke had seen exactly what he wanted him and the rest of Canela to see, a happy bridegroom. It was, as he had told Rachel, part of the plan. Convince the townspeople; impress the attorneys. As for the groom. . . .

Scott broke off that thought. Wiping his fingers on a paper napkin, he said calmly, "You know what they say: Prickly pears have soft interiors." And, oh, such soft lips. They had been his downfall. He should never have kissed her the way he did in that farmer's field. He had to make some sort of show; the other couple and the balloonist expected it. Newlyweds kissed. But there had been no reason for a full-fledged embrace.

Dumb. He had been dumb. He was so close to seeing his dream become reality. He already owned the station. That had been the first step. And the business was growing, prospering under his care. The next step was to gain the town's respect, to make them realize that Scott Sanders was a man to be reckoned with. He had almost achieved that, too. Last week he felt close enough that he almost tasted success. But now—now he couldn't afford a single mistake. He couldn't blow it now.

Br . . . rrr . . . ring. The kitchen phone made a loud, intrusive sound, startling Rachel as she unloaded the dishwasher. Leave it to Grandma to keep an old-fashioned phone with the volume set at maximum. She could imagine her grandmother's disapproving view of newfangled contraptions which trilled rather than rang. As for answering machines . . . Rachel made a mental note to buy one that afternoon.

"Oh, Rachel." Rachel's mild annoyance turned to fear when she heard her sister's voice. Becky's words were distorted, and she sounded as though she were crying. "Collapsed. Not breathing." Becky punctuated her words with sobs.

Rachel gripped the receiver, trying desperately not to panic. "What happened?" Something was wrong with Danny. She knew that. God willing, it was not as serious as Becky believed.

"I don't know." Becky's voice rose, and Rachel knew that her sister was close to the panic she herself was battling. "Rachel, please help me."

Rachel thought quickly. "We've got to get him to the hospital, and you can't drive." The last thing anyone needed was an hysterical Becky behind the wheel. "I'll call the paramedics and the doctor. Stay at home until they get there."

"I need you, Rachel."

"Don't worry. I'll be there." Rachel spoke slowly and firmly, trying to reassure her sister. "I'll meet you at the hospital. Now hang up, Becky, so I can call 911. Danny'll be fine."

She hoped.

As she drove toward the hospital, ignoring stop signs and speed limits, Rachel said a silent prayer that her optimism was founded. They were so close now, just weeks away from the surgery that would cure Danny's condition permanently. They couldn't lose him. They just couldn't.

Heedless of the prohibitive signs, Rachel left her car in the hospital director's spot then ran through the emergency room entrance.

"Danny Barton!" she cried as she reached the nurses' station. "Where is he?"

"ICU." One of the nurses gestured toward a door on the right. "Your sister's in there."

The waiting room was blessedly empty except for Becky. As Rachel ran inside, her sister flung her arms around Rachel and buried her head on her chest. "Oh, Rachel, I'm glad you're here. I'm so scared."

"Me, too." There was no point in lying. Rachel hugged her sister, then patted her back in a gesture of comfort. "We'll get through this. Doc Kingsley will take care of Danny. Didn't you tell me he's the best heart surgeon this side of Dallas?"

Rachel continued to talk about the future, about how healthy Danny would be. When Becky's tears subsided, Rachel led her to one of the faux leather couches. "Danny's got to be okay," Becky said. "I don't know what Tim and I would do if anything. . . . " She stopped, unwilling to put her fears into words.

"Where is Tim?" Rachel had expected to meet him in the waiting room. He should be here with his wife.

Becky wiped her eyes with a tissue. "Tim doesn't know about Danny. He had to go to Victoria this morning, and he'd already left when Danny got sick."

"Did you try his cell phone?"

Becky shook her head. "We don't have it any more. After we got the last hospital bills. . . . " Once again her voice trailed off, and Rachel sensed she was thinking about how tenuous their finances had been. In a year, they could have a dozen cell phones, but today—when it was critical—they had none.

"Do you know what happened to Danny?" When Rachel had seen him at her wedding, he appeared pale but otherwise healthy.

"I was doing dishes," Becky said, and the tears began to roll down her cheeks again. "Danny and Doxy were outside playing ball. I thought everything was fine until I heard the dog barking. She wouldn't stop, so I went out to see what was wrong." Rachel handed her sister another tissue. "Oh, Rachel," Becky sobbed, "I thought she might have chased a squirrel up a tree or something like that. Instead, there was Danny, lying on the ground."

It was awful feeling powerless, yet there was nothing she could say that would ease her sister's pain. Rachel put her arms around Becky, hoping the gesture would comfort her.

"Mrs. Barton."

The doctor was still in his surgical scrubs, the lines of fatigue scoring his face gave mute evidence of the severity of Danny's condition.

Becky jumped to her feet, and her voice trembled as she asked, "Is he okay? Is Danny fine?" She gripped Rachel's hand.

The doctor nodded slowly. "Your son is one lucky boy. We were able to stabilize him. But his heart is very weak."

Tears began to stream down Becky's cheeks, but this time Rachel knew they were tears of relief. "He's alive! Thank you, Doctor. Thank you." Becky managed a smile.

"Do you know what triggered today's attack?" It was Rachel who asked the question.

The doctor shook his head. "Excitement of some sort. I wouldn't want to speculate beyond that."

"Can I see him?" Becky asked tremulously.

"He's still sedated, but you can go into his room as soon as they move him out of Recovery. We'll need to keep him here for a few days' observation."

"What about his surgery?" Rachel formed the question that Becky was too distraught to remember.

Dr. Kingsley's frown worried Rachel as much as his words. "He's too weak to consider it now. We'll have to see how quickly he regains his strength." Though he didn't say the words, Rachel sensed that the doctor was warning them that Danny might not recover enough to undergo a major surgical procedure.

He looked so small, lying in the hospital bed, tubes in his arms and feet, his face almost as white as the sheets. But the nurses who stared at the monitors were smiling, and that, Rachel knew, meant that the crisis was over. For now.

"You can stay with him overnight, Mrs. Barton," one of the nurses said as Becky pulled a chair to Danny's bedside, putting her hand over one of his.

Becky looked up at Rachel, a question in her eyes.

"Don't worry. I'll get your things."

An hour later, when she was convinced Becky would be fine by herself, Rachel drove to her sister's house. She would pack an overnight bag, smuggling in some of the snacks her sister loved, which the hospital vending machines didn't stock. And, since it was unlikely Tim would remember, she would set out fresh food and water for the dog.

"Here, Doxy," she called as she entered the house. There was no answering bark, no sound of toenails clicking on the tile floors.

"Doxy?" Rachel walked quickly through the house, checking each of the small rooms. No dog. In all likelihood, Becky had put her outside. But the back yard was empty and a brief survey revealed the reason. Someone had left the gate open.

Just what Becky didn't need. If Danny knew his beloved dachshund was missing, he would be upset, and if there was one thing they couldn't afford, it was to have Danny upset. Not now.

The house was too quiet. He had expected the sound of music coming from the kitchen, for if there was one thing he'd learned about Rachel, it was that she liked music playing when she cooked.

"Rachel?"

The kitchen was empty. Not only was there no sign of dinner preparations, but the dishwasher was open, half-emptied, as if she'd left in a hurry. The faint unease he felt when he walked in the front door deepened.

"Rachel, where are you?" Her car was in the garage, and he doubted she'd walked anywhere. She had to be somewhere in the house, but why wasn't she answering his calls? Was she asleep? Or worse, was she hurt?

Quickly, Scott checked each of the first floor rooms, then climbed the stairs. It was then he heard the sobs; Rachel was crying as though her heart was broken. Something was horribly, horribly wrong. There was no denying the fear that gripped him or the adrenaline that surged through his veins.

Scott threw open the door to Rachel's room. "Rachel, honey, what's wrong?" His bride was sitting in a wicker chair next to the window, her face blotched from crying, tears streaming down her cheeks. She looked at him, her blue eyes filled with what appeared to be unbearable pain.

No! his heart screamed, but he kept his voice low and calm. "Are you hurt?" The sword of fear twisted, deeper and more painful than he would have believed possible. Rachel was ill. Someone had hurt her. Whatever had happened, he hadn't been there to comfort her. This last thought was somehow the most painful.

"What's wrong?" he asked again. She had to tell him. Surely whatever it was wasn't so horrible that she couldn't put it into words.

"It's Danny," she said. Slowly, her voice cracking from the strain, she told him what had happened. He could feel the terror that had gripped her from the moment Becky had called, and his heart ached to comfort her. He should have been with her. He would have, if only he'd known.

"Why didn't you call me?" he asked. "I would have come to the hospital."

For a second Rachel looked at him as though she didn't understand his question. Then her face flushed and she dropped her eyes. Her silence was more telling than any words would have been.

"It never occurred to you, did it?"

She turned to stare out the window rather than meet his gaze. It was more than Scott could bear. The woman who bore his name—if only temporarily—had completely forgotten his existence.

"What's wrong with you, Rachel?" he demanded, his voice harsh with anger, pain and fear—fear for them as well as Danny. "Don't you ever think of anyone other than yourself?"

She flinched as if he'd hit her. "I was thinking about my family," she said.

Her family. "What am I, chopped liver? In case you've forgotten, I'm your husband!"

Rachel jumped to her feet and faced him, her hands

fisted on her hips. "A husband in name only." Her voice was low but intense. "We're sharing a house, Scott, not a life."

The sword she had driven into his heart twisted, deepening the pain. Scott took a deep breath. "What about the gossip?" he demanded. "How do you think it looks when there's a family emergency and I'm not there? How do you explain that you've forgotten your husband of two days?"

"Stop it!" Rachel's cheeks flushed with anger. "You're just like my grandmother. You're trying to control me, trying to make me do what you want." She paused for a moment then added, "You keep attaching strings to everything."

Scott stared at her, struggling to understand her outburst. She had had a horrible day, the kind of day no one should have to endure alone. And yet . . . she just didn't understand.

"So you think I'm attaching strings, do you? I hate to tell you this, Rachel, but whether you like it or not, life comes with strings attached."

Chapter Six

She dressed with more care than normal that evening; they were having dinner with a couple Scott wanted to impress. When Rachel had asked who they were and why it was important that they thought well of Scott, he'd said only that they were business associates by the name of Wainscott. Whatever the reason, it was apparent that Scott wanted to show off his wife tonight, so she'd worn a dark blue silk dress that complimented both her eyes and her engagement ring.

Perhaps being with another couple would make this evening more enjoyable than the last few. Though Danny had proven remarkably resilient, recovering from his attack more quickly than the doctor expected, the tension marking Rachel's relationship with Scott had not eased. His sharp words still echoed in her mind, popping up when she least expected them. Though Scott treated her with civility, she could feel the anger emanating from him. At least she thought it was anger.

Tonight she wasn't sure, for he smiled as she descended the stairs. "Very nice," Scott said with an admiring glance at the soft skirt that swirled around her legs. This was the old Scott.

"You don't look so bad yourself," she returned, relieved that—if only for tonight—he appeared to be relaxed. Perhaps it was the change of clothes that changed his mood. Tonight Scott was wearing a dark suit that seemed oddly formal, compared to his normal jeans and tee shirts. Yet, as with the tuxedo he'd worn for their wedding, he appeared comfortable.

They drove to Victoria, which was halfway between Canela and the Wainscotts' home.

Though Scott had been mostly silent on the drive to Victoria, when they pulled into the parking lot next to the Wainscotts' Cadillac, he turned to Rachel, his smile so brilliant she caught her breath. "I hate sharing you with anyone tonight," he said in a low, intimate voice.

Before Rachel could respond, he jumped out of the car, then helped her out of the Mustang, entwining his fingers with hers as they walked toward the restaurant. Once inside, he kept a proprietary arm around her waist, then arranged the seating so that Rachel was next to him.

"I'd like you to meet my bride," Scott said to the gray-haired couple who joined them at the restaurant. Newlyweds, as Scott had told her more than once, were expected to provide public displays of affection. She knew that. She had even agreed. It was only that the contrast with their life at home was so extreme.

The restaurant was one of the most elegant in the area, with snowy white linens, delicately flocked wallpaper and a silver candelabra on each table. It was the perfect spot for a romantic dinner, hardly the place Rachel would have chosen for a business meeting. Still, George and Lila Wainscott appeared pleased by the choice.

"Remember when we first came here?" Lila asked with a fond glance at her husband. George patted her hand affectionately. After they ordered drinks and the waiter handed them large, leather-bound menus George turned to Scott. "I've heard good things about you," he said. "The word is you're a man who's going places."

Rachel managed a light laugh. "And here I thought he was going to settle down."

As the Wainscotts chuckled, Scott pressed a light kiss on her cheek. "Don't worry, sweetheart. They couldn't pry me out of Canela these days," he said. "Not with you waiting for me at home. No, George, my roving days are over." And he kissed Rachel again.

She blushed. Though she knew it was only for show, Rachel wasn't accustomed to Scott's intimate tone or his kisses. He might be a superb actor, but she had yet to master the art.

"I stand corrected." George peered over his reading glasses. "I should have said you're a man who's going to do things."

"I certainly hope so, sir. You know I've got lots of plans, and I'm not afraid of hard work."

As George nodded, Lila gave Rachel a long appraising look. "You made a good choice in your husband," she said. "He's a hard worker, a good provider."

"Not like many of the younger generation." There was no mistaking the scorn in George's voice. "Too many young people expect things to be given to them. They don't want to wait or work."

Scott closed his menu and looked directly at George, his face a study in sincerity. "Rachel and I believe in earning our own way," he told the older man. "I guess you could say we don't believe in free lunches."

Rachel's eyes widened ever so slightly. Was Scott—the man who agreed to marry her so that he'd get half a million dollars—actually saying he worked for everything?

George laughed and snapped his menu closed. "I suppose this means you expect Lila and me to pay for our dinner."

It was Scott's turn to laugh. "My mother would turn over in her grave if she thought that was how I treated my guests."

"Well, then, Lila," George said with another affectionate pat on his wife's hand. "Feel free to order the lobster."

While Lila and Rachel discussed the waiter's suggestions, George began grilling Scott about his expansion plans for the station. Though Rachel would have liked to hear what the men were saying, she didn't want to be rude to Lila, who was debating the merits of prime rib and chicken cordon bleu. Besides, Rachel could hardly admit that she knew nothing of her husband's plans. It was obvious Lila, who seemed to take a deep interest in George's business, would not understand if Scott had not confided in his wife.

As soon as the main course was served, George turned the conversation to lighter topics, and Rachel found herself enjoying the evening. George and Lila had a wry sense of humor that appealed to her, and Scott was every inch the charming host. If only he would stop caressing her hand and pressing soft kisses on her cheek! George and Lila seemed to find it amusing, but that was not the adjective she would have chosen. Disturbing, annoying, embarrassing. Any of them was closer to the truth. It was not amusing.

"Well, my boy," George said when Scott signed the credit card slip and they prepared to leave, "I don't mind telling you I like what I saw and heard tonight." He looked at Lila, and she nodded. "My lawyers will call yours next week."

Scott beamed.

"All right," Rachel said when they were in the car headed back to Canela. "Who are they and what was that all about?"

The sun had set, and a crescent moon lit the sky. Though it was a beautiful evening, the splendor was lost on Rachel. She felt like a fool, not knowing why Scott wanted to impress the Wainscotts.

"George is a potential investor," Scott told her, his voice low and even, as if he were oblivious to her anger. "He won't make any decisions without Lila's approval. Says he sets a lot of store in families. That's why he wanted to meet you."

"Investor?" Rachel focused on Scott's first statement. "Why do you need an investor? Isn't half a million enough?"

The lights of the oncoming cars played on Scott's face, and she could see him shake his head. "I don't have that money yet," he reminded her. "And I can't afford to wait a year to start the station's expansion.

What I told George was the truth: every month without the new pumps puts me that much further behind."

Rachel thought quickly, trying to remember the exact wording of her grandmother's will.

"Maybe you don't have to wait. I'll call Mr. Dundee tomorrow morning. There has to be a way you can get the money earlier."

"Don't even think about it!" Scott practically shouted the words.

It was not the reaction she had expected. "What's wrong?" she asked, surprised by his anger. Why should he object to getting his money early? It made no sense, unless. . . . "Have you suddenly developed scruples?" she asked. "Or did you start believing what you told George about earning your own way? That was quite a speech about no free lunches."

Scott grabbed her arm. "Is this your way of telling me you don't think I'm earning my money?" he demanded, his voice harsh with anger.

"The question isn't what I think but what George thinks. Isn't that right?" Rachel pried Scott's fingers from her arm and slid as far away from him as the small car would permit. "I've agreed that you'll get the money, and—to be very honest—I think you deserve it. That's why I want to see if Mr. Dundee will release it early."

"No!"

"No one would need to know."

"Rachel, I said no, and I mean it. Leave it alone!" Scott's hands gripped the steering wheel so tightly Rachel could see the leather flex. It was obvious he felt strongly about this, but it still made no sense.

"Why? I don't understand why you'd take George's money but not your own."

Scott was silent for a long moment. When he spoke, his voice was fierce. "The station is mine. Whether it's a success or failure depends on me. And me alone. I don't need your help."

It was odd how the words hurt. They shouldn't have. After all, what difference did it make whether Scott took his share of the inheritance now or in a year? They had a business arrangement. That was all. It wasn't as though she felt a need or even a desire to help him. But no one liked rejection, and Scott had just dealt her a big one.

"Maybe I want to help you." She was surprised when the words tumbled out, seemingly of their own volition.

Scott took a deep breath, and Rachel sensed that he was trying to rein in his temper. "Why would you want to do that? Is this your idea of being the bountiful lady of the manor or something?" Scott's voice was harsh. Without giving her a chance to reply, he continued, "Whatever your reason, I'm not buying it. After all, you're the one who told me—pretty emphatically as I recall—that we share nothing more than a house."

They were her own words, and, oh, did they hurt. Almost as much as Scott's calling her self-centered.

It was amazing how little there was to do. For as long as she could remember, her days had been filled, first with school, then with work. Now there was a void. For the first time in her life, Rachel was bored. She couldn't spend every day with Becky and Danny.

That wasn't fair to them. She ought to get a job, but there weren't many available in Canela, and it seemed unfair to take one when someone else needed the pay and she didn't. Still, she wanted—no, she needed—something to fill her days.

When the phone rang, a soft trill from the new answering machine in the kitchen, Rachel ran to pick it up. Even if it was a vinyl siding salesman, at least she would have someone to talk to for a few minutes.

"Good morning, sister of mine."

Rachel laughed, knowing what was coming. Becky was so predictable. "What do you need today?" she asked. Whenever Becky addressed her as "sister," it was because she had a favor to beg.

"Not today," her sister said with a chuckle. "Saturday. Would you mind baby-sitting so Tim and I can go out to dinner?"

Would she mind? Hardly. An evening with Danny was far preferable to staying home and watching reruns on TV while Scott made his saccharine calls to Justine. If she had to hear his low, intimate voice and those disgustingly sweet words he used with Justine one more time, she'd be sick. Though a normally sensible man, Scott certainly had a blind spot where Justine was concerned. It was as though every shred of reason deserted him when he started talking to her.

But Rachel didn't want to think about Scott and Justine. She smiled as she answered her sister, "You know I'd be glad to baby-sit. Any reason is a good one. But tell me, Becky, does this mean that Danny's back to normal?" Becky and Tim hadn't left their son alone since he'd returned from the hospital.

Rachel stared out the window, scarcely noticing the

two birds splashing contentedly in the old-fashioned birdbath.

"He's not completely recovered," Becky admitted, "but he's much better. Now that Doxy's home, Danny's one happy boy."

"And you still have no idea where the dog went." Doxy had been gone for a few hours, returning home slightly bedraggled, ravenously hungry, but otherwise apparently no worse for her adventure. Everyone was worried because Doxy was expecting soon.

One of the birds dipped its head into the water, then shook it furiously. "No. But the vet confirmed she's fine and so are the puppies." Rachel heard Becky sigh. "I know Danny will be thrilled by the thought of puppies, but I'm not sure I'm ready for this."

Rachel laughed, remembering Becky had said the same thing when she became pregnant with Danny. "At least your life isn't boring."

"And yours is?"

"You could say that." Though her sister couldn't see her, Rachel nodded. "Becky, I'm going to go crazy if I don't find something to do. I can only spend so many hours at the country club, and my nails don't need to be polished daily." She frowned at the perfectly-shaped acrylic nails. Though they were beautiful and made her hands look elegant, Rachel thought of them as "lady of leisure" nails, reminding her of how Scott had called her self-centered.

"I thought about volunteering as a teacher's aide," Rachel continued, "but talk about bad timing. It's summer, and school's out."

Becky was silent for a moment. "What about Magnolia Gardens?" she asked at last, referring to the nursing home on the other side of town. "The patients love visitors, and I've heard there's always a shortage of people to spend time with them."

"Magnolia Gardens?" That possibility had not occurred to Rachel. "What on earth would I say to them?" she asked.

Becky hooted. "Is this my sister talking? I can't imagine you being at a loss for words. Besides, the patients talk, too. Think about it."

And Rachel did. No doubt about it, working at a nursing home wasn't her first choice. Her only experience with older people had been living with her grandmother, and that was hardly good preparation for amiable relationships with a different generation. Still, it would help fill the void in her life. And, though not her primary motivation, it would stop Scott from telling her she was self-centered.

Rachel changed into a pair of gray linen slacks and a lighter gray silk blouse. Then, seeing her reflection in the mirror, she frowned. Gray was definitely not the color to wear to Magnolia Gardens. She pulled out the navy suit and hot pink T-shirt that she'd worn for her lunch with Brad Stewart. At least it was bright and cheerful.

"Rachel Fleming." Mrs. Nelson, the administrator of Magnolia Gardens looked up from her desk, unable to hide her surprise, although she tried to camouflage it with a quick laugh.

"I'm sorry. It's Rachel Sanders now, isn't it?" She shook Rachel's hand and motioned her to one of the chairs by her round conference table. "What brings you here?"

Rachel swallowed. This was more difficult than she

had expected. Though she had applied for jobs, she had never before volunteered. What would she do if Mrs. Nelson refused her? "I understand you need aides."

"And you want to be one?"

Mrs. Nelson gave Rachel a long appraising look, as though she needed to assure herself of Rachel's intentions. "If you're sure, we have one woman in her early eighties," she said at last. "She broke her leg last week and is in traction, so she's pretty lonely. Her children aren't in the area, and most of her friends are already gone." The administrator paused again. "If you're interested, I know Mrs. Thomas would appreciate companionship."

Rachel's heart went out to the bedridden woman. How awful! But what would she say to her? No matter what Becky said, Rachel wasn't sure she knew how to converse with seniors.

Forcing a smile onto her face and hoping her nervousness didn't show, Rachel followed Mrs. Nelson down the long, sunny corridor from the common rooms to the patients' individual bedrooms. After seeing exposés about nursing homes on TV, Rachel was surprised by how pleasant the surroundings were. Not only were the rooms bright with sunlight from the large windows and skylights, but they were tastefully decorated in cheerful colors.

"Mrs. Thomas, this is Rachel Flem—er, Sanders. She's come to see you," Mrs. Nelson said as they entered one of the rooms. Though painted the same shade of yellow as Rachel's bedroom, instead of a canopied bed, this room was dominated by a hospital bed with traction apparatus.

The woman lying in the bed, her leg encased in white plaster, was tiny, with bones that looked so fragile Rachel hesitated to shake her hand. But Mary Thomas's grip was firm, and her smile told Rachel she was indeed happy to have a visitor.

"Call me Mary," she said when the administrator had left them alone. She gestured toward the upholstered chair which stood in one corner of her room.

"Bring the chair closer," Mary said in her firm voice. "My eyes aren't as good as they once were." Rachel wasn't sure she believed the protest, for Mrs. Thomas's blue eyes appeared alert and filled with intelligence, but she placed the chair next to the bed.

"Would you like me to read you a book or maybe play a game with you?" Mrs. Nelson had indicated those were the activities most patients preferred.

Mary Thomas shook her head. "Nonsense. My eyes may not be as good as yours, but I can still read." She patted Rachel's hand. "What I can't do is talk to myself. That's what I miss the most here: conversation. So, tell me about yourself."

Becky was wrong if she thought Rachel was rarely at a loss for words. Her own life was not a topic Rachel enjoyed discussing. Particularly not her life since she returned to Canela.

"Well. . . ." She thought for a moment, trying to decide what to say. "I recently moved back here."

Mary nodded, as if encouraging her to continue. Her sharp blue gaze moved from Rachel's face to her hands. "You're married," she said, "and if my eyes don't deceive me, that ring is new."

"Right on both counts." Rachel forced a cheerful tone into her voice. "I came back to Canela to get married." *Because I had to*, she added silently, *although not for the reason most people mean when they say that.*

Mary lay back on her pillow and closed her eyes for a moment, concentrating on something. "What did you say your name was?" she asked as she opened her eyes again.

"Rachel Sanders." It still sounded odd.

"Not that one. What was your maiden name?"

"Fleming."

Mary smiled triumphantly. "I thought you looked familiar," she crowed. "Now I know why. You remind me of Laura Fleming."

"You knew my grandmother?" She shouldn't have been surprised. Mary Thomas was a few years older than her grandmother, but they were definitely the same generation, and Canela was a town where there were few strangers.

"Indeed, I did know her. We used to play bridge together every month."

How well Rachel remembered the months when her grandmother's bridge club had met at their house. Those months she and Becky had done a particularly thorough cleaning, polishing every piece of silver and crystal in the house, although—as Rachel had pointed out to her grandmother on numerous occasions—no one used the crystal.

"To tell you the truth," Mary said, bringing Rachel firmly back to the present, "we all used to get a little tired of listening to Laura talk."

"Are we talking about the same Laura Fleming?" Rachel couldn't help asking the question, for her grandmother had been a silent, almost dour woman, except, of course, for the times when she had felt compelled to lecture Rachel on her responsibilities. Then she had not lacked for words.

"Oh, lordy, yes." Mary Thomas nodded emphatically to underscore her words. "You couldn't stop her once she started talking about you and your sister. She was so proud of you."

It was Rachel's turn to nod. "That was Becky. She always was the biddable granddaughter." How many times had Rachel heard her grandmother extol Becky's virtues and ask Rachel why she couldn't be more like her sister?

Mary shook her head. "No, my dear. You were the one she talked about the most. Laura was so proud of your spirit. She used to call you her feisty one and tell us how worried she was about raising you properly."

Feisty. That was a word Rachel had never heard on her grandmother's lips. "She tried her best." Rachel couldn't deny that. While she may not have agreed with her grandmother's methods, she couldn't claim that her motives had been wrong.

At Mary's request, Rachel poured her a glass of water. When she had taken a sip, the older woman continued her reminiscing. Rachel would have stopped her—she had no desire to revive memories of her grandmother—but it was obvious Mary was enjoying her role as raconteur. Only a selfish person, Rachel reminded herself, would put her own comfort ahead of another's pleasure.

"Why, I remember the year you refused to have a birthday cake," Mary said. "You insisted you would only eat cheesecake, and they had to be individual servings." She laughed. "Poor Laura. She wasn't much of a baker."

"In today's parlance, we'd call her 'cooking challenged.'" Fortunately, Becky had shown a flair in the kitchen and had started preparing their meals when she was a teenager.

Mary took another sip of water, then placed the glass on the bedside stand. "Your grandmother searched everywhere for a cheesecake recipe that was easy enough for her to make. We all thought she was foolish and told her she ought to order one from the bakery, but she wouldn't listen."

"Grandma was a stubborn woman."

"Now, child, I'd prefer to call her determined," Mary said with a reproving pat to Rachel's hand. "Laura was determined that you'd have a homemade cheesecake. I don't remember who finally found the recipe, but I do recall how happy she was when you asked for a second helping." The older woman shook her head. "We had to listen to that story for four months running. You'd have thought someone had given her the Nobel Peace Prize or something."

Proud of her. Happy because of something she had done. Those were not words Rachel would have attributed to her grandmother, and yet that was how Mary Thomas remembered her. Perhaps time had colored Mary's memory.

Rachel could never remember Grandma Laura expressing approval. As for the cheesecake, not once did her grandmother so much as hint that she had had any difficulty in making it. She had simply arranged the small cakes in a circle, decorated them with candles, then placed them on the table in front of Rachel and told her to make a wish before she ate one. Grandma had treated it as though it were an ordinary cake, not something that had caused her days of preparation.

Mary seemed so confident of her memory that Rachel found it difficult to dismiss her tale. And why should she? It was a small, probably insignificant event in her grandmother's life. There was no reason to assign undue importance to it. But if Mary's story was true, it raised another, far more serious, question. Were there other things Rachel didn't know about her grandmother?

Chapter Seven

"Your table is ready, Mr. Sanders." The maitre d' led them to a round table in the center of Canela's finest restaurant. Small and intimate, the dining room held only half a dozen tables, and reservations, particularly at this time of the year, had to be made months in advance. Rachel wasn't sure how Scott had managed to get them a table on such short notice, but she suspected it was part of Scott's campaign to keep them in the public eye, his "convince the lawyers" strategy.

As he pulled out Rachel's chair and seated her, Scott's hand lingered for a moment at the small of her back. The man was definitely acting again, pretending they were a happily married couple, not two strangers who shared a house.

When the waiter, who introduced himself as Michael, had opened their menus and explained the daily specials, Scott placed his hand over Rachel's. "I imagine Canela seems boring after the big city." His words were cool, contrasting with the warmth that spread up her arm as his fingers caressed hers. It was all for show, she reminded herself. There was no reason her pulse should race or her face should flush.

A second later Rachel remembered Scott's question. "It's not as bad as it was at first," she admitted, surprised when she realized the truth of her words. The days no longer seemed to drag. In fact, there were times—like today—when she wished they lasted more than twenty-four hours.

"Then you enjoy Magnolia Gardens?"

Indeed she did. The time she spent with Mary Thomas had become one of the highlights of her days. As she nodded, Scott smiled. "I'm glad."

"Why should you care?"

Scott shrugged and studied the menu as though it contained the mysteries of the universe. "My life's a lot easier when you're happy," he said at last.

The dining room was full by the time the waiter brought their appetizers, and so Rachel attached no importance to the fact that Michael was followed by a second waiter. As Michael set the shrimp cocktail in front of Rachel and Scott, the second waiter placed a huge bouquet of early summer flowers next to Rachel. "For you, Madame," he said with a formal bow.

Rachel stared at the flowers. Since each of the tables had a single yellow rose next to the silver candlestick, they obviously weren't part of the restaurant's decor.

Scott leaned closer to her. "Happy anniversary, darling." He placed his hand on the back of her neck and gently touched her lips with his. It was the softest of kisses, as light as the brush of a feather, and yet it stirred her senses.

"Anniversary?" she asked, trying to still the pounding of her heart.

Scott's smile was as soft as his kiss. "Don't tell me you haven't been counting. Today's our one-month anniversary." Rachel flushed. She had not been counting! But Scott didn't seem to mind. He brought her fingers to his lips and kissed them.

"Thank you, sweetheart, for the happiest month of my life." Though Scott spoke softly, his words were clear, and Rachel heard the couples at the two tables closest to them start to murmur. Rachel flushed again. The man was making a spectacle of them! It was one thing to pretend, but this was going too far. Scott may have had a mother who believed in public displays of affection, but Rachel had been taught to abhor them.

She dipped her shrimp into the cocktail sauce, trying to concentrate on the perfectly prepared food rather than Scott's words and actions. The flowers were beautiful. With some luck the Canela grapevine would focus on them rather than Scott's kiss and romantic words. And maybe pigs would fly.

Rachel's eyes widened, for when Michael returned with the Caesar salad Scott had ordered, he was once again followed by the second waiter. This time he handed Scott a large heart-shaped box.

Flowers and now this! As the other diners stared, obviously enthralled by the drama being played out at the Sanders table, Scott rose, then knelt next to Rachel, holding out the box that could only contain candy. "Sweets, my dear, to remind you that you're the sweetest thing in my life." The silence in the dining room ensured that everyone heard his words.

Scott reached for Rachel's hand. Turning it over, he placed a kiss on her palm. While his first kiss had been brief, this one lingered, sending sparks of pleasure up her arm. How embarrassing! She was blushing like a teenager. For the briefest of moments Rachel wondered how she would feel if Scott were her husband in more than name, if the gifts, the pretty words and the kisses were real, not simply part of an elaborate charade. But, of course, none of it was real, so it was foolish to indulge in such pointless fantasies.

Somehow Rachel managed a normal conversation as she and Scott ate their salads, when all the while she wondered what was next.

To Rachel's surprise, when Michael brought their steaks, he was alone. She had started to think that Scott had planned a gift for each course. Obviously, she was wrong. How typical. Just when she thought she understood Scott, he proved that she didn't.

But the huge tray contained three covered plates. Michael removed the covers, revealing two steaks and a gaily wrapped square package. Scott handed her the package, grinning as she felt the edges.

"A book."

"They're kind of hard to camouflage," he said with another grin.

As she tore off the wrappings, Rachel's smile turned into a full-fledged grin of her own. "Diane Roberts! She's my favorite author!"

"I kind of thought so. That row of dog-eared paperbacks was a bit of a giveaway."

"Oh, Scott, I can't wait to read this one. Everyone says it's her best yet." Rachel stared at the brightly colored dustcover, admiring the fanciful lettering that proclaimed this the latest star in Diane Roberts' ever growing constellation of romances.

"Why don't you read a page or two?" Scott suggested.

It was an odd request. Who would read a book in a fancy restaurant, particularly when the main course had just been served? But Rachel needed no further urging. She opened the book and turned to the title page.

"An autographed copy! Oh, Scott! This is wonderful."

"Worth a kiss?" he asked.

Rachel raised a brow. *Why not?* It wasn't as though they had had a low profile dinner and—even if the gifts were all for show—Scott had gone to a lot of trouble to plan them. The least she could do was play her part.

"Sure." Rachel leaned toward Scott and pressed her lips to his. Her grandmother would definitely have disapproved of the public display of affection, but she would have been equally disapproving of Rachel's cries of delight over the book. Emotions, Grandma had always declared, were to be controlled, not displayed like Monday's laundry. Fortunately, pleasing Grandma was no longer on Rachel's priority list.

"Flowers, books, candy. Those are very proper gifts," Rachel said as she sliced a piece of the succulent beef. "My grandmother would have approved." *And there wasn't much that met her standards*, Rachel added silently.

She most definitely would not have approved of dessert, for as Michael brought the cherries jubilee to their table, the second waiter followed with a large box covered with silver paper and a huge silver bow.

"I can't imagine what's in it," Rachel told Scott. "We've run out of Victorian gifts."

"Then I guess it's a good thing we don't live in Victorian times." Scott raised one brow and gestured toward the box. "Aren't you just a little curious to see what's inside?"

As Rachel unfolded the tissue paper and saw Scott's gift, she could feel the blood rush to her face, for the box held a negligee, a delicate concoction of silk and lace. Hurriedly, she stuffed it back into the box, but not before she heard the people at the next table titter.

Without giving Rachel time to react, Scott pulled her to her feet and wrapped his arms around her. Lowering his head to hers, he kissed her . . . a long, slow kiss that caused Rachel's blush to deepen. When at length he released her, the other diners began to applaud.

"Bravo! Do it again!"

But, of course, Scott did not. He had done enough to convince the other patrons that he and Rachel were happy newlyweds.

"This is beginning to seem like mission impossible." Scott scribbled a note on the sheet of paper in front of him, then crumpled it and tossed it at the wastebasket. In keeping with the kind of day he was having, it missed.

"What's wrong, besides the fact that the Chicago Bulls aren't likely to recruit you?" Though Luke's words were light, his face was uncustomarily solemn as he stood in the doorway of the small office, holding a newspaper in one hand, a coffee mug in the other.

Scott looked up. "I'm surrounded by three feet of

paper, I've been pulling my hair out by the handful, and you want to know what's wrong. Gimme a break, Luke." He crumpled another sheet of paper, then raised a fist in victory when it landed inside the wastebasket. "It's those cursed permit applications. That's what's wrong." With a quick look at his watch, he groused, "I don't think the actual construction will take as long as the paperwork, and there's definitely something wrong with that picture."

Luke shifted his weight from one foot to the other and then back. "I don't think you're gonna like what I have to tell you," he said when Scott demanded to know what was going on.

"Let me guess. You're going to take that vacation you've been threatening to the same week construction starts. Go ahead. Go see that uncle of yours in New Jersey or wherever it is that he lives."

Luke shook his head. "It's not that easy." He rolled the newspaper then slapped the wall with it. "There's been a big leak at Walter's station." Though his station was in the next county, Walter Gross was Scott's biggest rival. Scott's rotten day had just gotten substantially worse.

"Tell me it wasn't the underground tanks." The words were more a plea than a command.

Luke shuffled his feet, clearly uneasy. "Do you want me to lie?" he asked and raised his eyes to meet Scott's gaze. "If so, of course it wasn't the underground tanks." Luke slapped the wall again. "The truth is, Walter didn't have proper containment, so now there's a major cleanup and the threat of remediation."

This was worse than almost anything Scott could

have imagined. "Let me guess. There's also a media feeding frenzy."

"Right on the first try. If your stomach's really strong, take a look at this." Luke handed him the paper with its front page coverage of the leak.

Scott's reaction was succinct, predictable and totally unprintable. "I didn't need this," he said as he reread the inflammatory comments that accompanied the story. "After this, the agency'll be stricter than ever. They'll make me dot every *i*, and they'll review every page twenty times instead of the usual fifteen." Scott rested his head in his hands. "I really didn't need this. Now there's no telling when they'll approve the permits."

Though he left the words unspoken, Scott knew there was the very real possibility that the agency, in its zeal to prevent a future leak, would not approve the permits at all. If that happened, he would not be able to expand the station, and his dream would never come true.

"You could try bribing the review team," Luke suggested. "Rumor has it that's how Walter got away without the containment beds."

Scott's head jerked up, and he could feel the adrenaline course through his veins. "Don't even think it," he said, his voice low and fierce as he tried to control his anger. "You know me better than that."

Luke nodded. "Yeah, I do. Straight Arrow Sanders."

"He looks good." Rachel's eyes followed her nephew as he once again played catch with the brown dachshund. Danny's face no longer bore a hospital pallor, and he seemed to be running with less difficulty, enjoying his backyard almost like a normal child.

"Dr. Kingsley is pleased," Becky confirmed. She leaned back in the lawn chair, more relaxed than Rachel had seen her in weeks. "He thinks we may be able to schedule surgery in a month."

It was welcome news, for the doctor had originally feared that it might be three or four months before Danny would be strong enough to undergo surgery.

"What about the dog?"

Becky laughed. "We're pretty sure she's pregnant, but we haven't told Danny yet."

Rachel did some mental arithmetic. "So the puppies would be due right around Danny's surgery. Good timing. It'll give him something to do while he's recovering."

"Everything's working out." Becky's grin reinforced her positive words. "Some days I can hardly believe it, but it seems like all my dreams are coming true."

It had been a long time since Rachel had seen her sister so happy. In fact, happy seemed too tame a word to describe her. Becky was almost euphoric. "There's something else, isn't there? Something more than Danny and the puppies."

Becky leaned forward and touched Rachel's hand. "I never could keep secrets from you, could I?" She squeezed Rachel's fingers. "You're right, sister of mine. There is something else." Becky paused, and Rachel knew it was a deliberate move, designed to heighten her suspense. Becky took a sip of coffee, then announced, "Tim and I have decided to have another baby."

A baby.

"Are you sure?" When Danny had been born with his serious heart problems, Becky had confided that she and Tim were afraid to have another child.

Becky nodded. "I'd be lying if I said we didn't have worries. Any sane person would. But Danny's problem isn't hereditary, and we think he needs a sibling." Becky's eyes were serious as she looked at her sister. "Who am I trying to kid? Tim and I need a second child. We're having this baby for us, not Danny. But, oh, Rachel, wouldn't it be great if our babies were due at the same time?"

"Our babies?" What was Becky talking about? Rachel wasn't going to have a baby, not now, probably not ever. She opened her mouth to tell Becky that a baby was impossible without a second immaculate conception, but clamped her jaw closed instead. She couldn't tell anyone—not even her sister—that her marriage was a sham.

Seemingly oblivious to Rachel's discomfort, Becky said, "You're the biggest news Canela's had in a long time. It happens every time I turn around at the bank, the cleaners, the supermarket, you name it. No one misses a chance to tell me how much Scott loves you." Becky shrugged. "I've heard there's even a pool so people can bet on the day you two announce you're pregnant."

Things were definitely getting out of hand.

"Is something wrong?" Scott swallowed his last bite of cherry pie, then pushed the plate away.

For a moment Rachel stared at him. She knew she was in a bad mood, but who wouldn't be after Becky's revelations? This marriage arrangement was turning out to be far more complicated than she had ever dreamed. Leave it to Grandma to mess up her life even from the grave.

"What could be wrong?" Rachel asked, her voice dripping with sarcasm. "The whole town's speculating on when our baby's due, but why should that bother me?"

If her words surprised him, Scott gave no evidence; he merely regarded her steadily. "You tell me, Rachel." He turned the question around. "Why should that bother you? I'd have thought you'd be happy that everyone was convinced we had a normal marriage. Now no one will think about contesting the will."

Rachel knew her reaction was irrational, but that didn't stop her from lashing out at Scott. "Would you stop being reasonable?"

His lips thinned, and she could see the anger simmering just below the surface. Scott shoved his chair back. "Fine. I've got work to do, anyway. If you need me, I'll be in the den."

Rachel's mood did not improve as she cleared the table and loaded the dishwasher. Normally Scott helped her with the kitchen chores, telling her it was the least he could do when she did all the cooking. But tonight, thanks to her outburst, he had left her alone. She measured the detergent, pushed the start button, then switched off the lights. The pots and pans would have to wait until tomorrow. In her current frame of mind, she would be more likely to bang than to scrub them.

She started to climb the stairs, then changed her mind. Just because Scott wanted to use the den didn't mean that he owned it. She would pop a favorite movie into the VCR and escape to a world where happy endings were guaranteed.

"Everyone's talking about babies." Rachel clenched her fists as she realized Scott was making yet another of his calls to Justine. Couldn't the man skip one night? "I can't wait until we're having one of our own." He paused, and Rachel knew Justine was murmuring something. "Just the thought of that life growing inside you . . . oh, sweetheart. . . ."

Disgusted, Rachel turned away. How could Justine stand it? Not just the sickeningly-sweet words Scott used whenever he called her, but the whole situation. The man Justine loved was married to another woman, and she couldn't see him for a year. For the hundredth time, Rachel wondered what sort of woman Justine was that she would have agreed to this marriage. Oh, there was the promise of a beautiful house bought with the money Scott would receive, but Rachel knew that she would prefer the smallest of apartments rather than let her fiancé live with another woman. And even the hours and hours of phone calls Scott made were no substitute for being together.

I wonder just how much time he has spent talking to her, Rachel thought. There was an easy way to find out. Returning to the kitchen, she opened her small desk and pulled out the unpaid bills. The one from the phone company would tell her how many hours Scott had spent talking to Justine.

When she opened it, Rachel's frustration ratcheted up another level. "I can't tell you how much I appreciate your sensitivity." She stood at the door to the den brandishing the phone bill.

"I'll call you back," Scott murmured to Justine. When he'd hung up, he rose and turned to Rachel. "This seems to be your night for sarcasm, but you'll have to excuse me if I don't have a clue what you're talking about."

She took a step into the room. "This," she said, waving the bill in front of him. "There are no phone calls to Houston, so I assume you've been reversing the charges."

"You assume wrong."

His low, matter-of-fact tone inflamed Rachel further. "Don't tell me you're going to try to deny that you made all those calls to Justine."

"I wouldn't even try—especially when you've been so busy eavesdropping on my private conversations."

Rachel flinched at the criticism. He was right, but still . . . "Okay. So you admit you made the calls, and you say you didn't reverse the charges. We both know the phone company isn't a charitable institution, which means those calls weren't free."

"I never said they were." Scott took a step toward Rachel, and the look in his eyes made her move back. Had she thought he was calm? About as calm as a geyser about to erupt. "What I have said—more than once as I recall—is that I don't ask my women to pay my way."

Rachel stared at him. He was angry, no doubt about that, but surely the anger was out of proportion to the cause?

"What's the matter, Rachel? Haven't you ever heard of third party billing?" It was Scott's turn for sarcasm. "It's quite simple, really. I charge the calls to the station's number. Now, if you'll leave me alone, I have a few things to discuss with Justine." He reached for the phone.

"Like picking out names for the baby you want to have?"

Scott shrugged. "Not everyone's like you, Rachel. Believe it or not, Justine likes the idea of having babies with me."

Chapter Eight

She was surprised at her own reaction. Who would have thought she'd find such pleasure in making plans for Canela's annual Fourth of July celebration? As a child, she had looked forward to the parade, the amusement rides and the fireworks, while she and Becky had dreaded the seemingly endless speeches. But she was no longer a child, and hadn't expected to enjoy the town's premier event. Yet here she was, humming patriotic songs as she tucked a red-and-white gingham shirt into her jeans skirt.

"I'm surprised you could close the station today," Rachel said as she and Scott drove to her sister's house. Since parking was always at a premium, they had decided that the five of them—plus the dog, of course—would go in Becky and Tim's van. "Aren't there always a lot of people needing gas at the last minute?"

"You bet." Scott shifted into a lower gear to pass a truck. "We couldn't close the station, so Luke's working today. He volunteers to work every holiday."

"For the triple pay?"

Scott shook his head. "Oh, Luke doesn't turn that down, but I don't think that's the reason. Being at work means he doesn't have to see all the families."

"You mean he hasn't put the memories behind him?" Rachel knew about Luke's wife's and daughter's deaths but had thought that the worst of the grief was over.

"Apparently not. He doesn't talk about it."

And you'd rather not, either, Rachel surmised from Scott's terse tone. She changed the subject, chattering about unimportant things until they pulled into Becky's driveway. Though there was no sign of her sister or Tim, Danny sat on the front porch, clearly waiting for them.

"Look, Uncle Scott!" Danny raced toward the car, trailed closely by his dog. "Look! Doxy's got a ribbon. It's red, white and boo."

As he stepped out, Scott ruffled the boy's hair. "I think that's 'blue'," he said gently.

"Blue." Danny repeated the word. "Thanks, Uncle Scott."

Uncle Scott. How odd that sounded. For a moment Rachel wanted to correct Danny, to tell him that Scott wasn't really his uncle. But she couldn't, for Danny was the reason Scott was pretending to be an uncle, a brother-in-law, and a husband. And if he was none of those at the end of the year, at least Danny would have his surgery.

Seconds later Becky and Tim emerged from the house, raising Danny's excitement level. As they strapped him into his car seat and settled the dog next to him, Becky turned to Rachel. "I'm glad you're home again," she said.

"So am I." Scott, who had been helping Tim load picnic supplies into the back, materialized at Rachel's side. He slid his arm around her waist and drew her near, pressing a quick kiss on her hair before helping her climb into the van. "This is the best July Fourth I can remember," he told Becky as the van rolled down the driveway, "and your sister is the reason."

"Rachel, what did you do in Dallas?" Becky asked as Tim turned onto the main road. "Did you go to the fireworks?"

Rachel shook her head. "My friend Megan's family has a cottage on a small lake. We'd have a barbecue and some fireworks there, but what I remember most was the sunburn." And the fact that for three years Megan had tried matchmaking between Rachel and her brother. Neither of them had been interested, but that hadn't stopped Megan. Her matchmaking had continued up to the moment that her brother had moved east.

They arrived at the fairgrounds early enough to get seats in the grandstand. Once they were settled, Scott put his arm around Rachel's shoulders and drew her against him. "Space is at a premium," he whispered in her ear when she started to draw back. "Besides, don't forget those lawyers." Rachel forced her lips to turn up in a smile. There was no telling how many people were looking in their direction, and she couldn't afford to let them see how uncomfortable she was.

Once the parade started, Rachel's smile became genuine. Who wouldn't enjoy watching Danny watch the floats? He clapped his hands in glee at the clowns and informed Aunt Rachel and Uncle Scott that he was going to learn to turn cartwheels just like the cheerleaders.

But once the speeches began, Danny's attention wandered. So too did Scott's, or so it seemed, for he began to nibble Rachel's earlobe.

"Stop that!" she hissed, as disturbed by the shivers of pleasure that swept through her as she was by Scott's public show of affection.

"If you turn your head," he whispered, unrepentant, "I'll see if the other one is as tasty."

"Not on your life!" It was surprising how hard it was to argue with Scott while she kept a smile on her face. If they were at home, she could tell him exactly how she felt. Of course, if they were at home, he wouldn't be making this display.

"Why are you eating Aunt Rachel's ear?"

As waves of embarrassment swept over her, Rachel was sure her face matched her gingham shirt. Scott, it appeared, was not in the least chagrined. "I was *kissing* her," he explained, "and that's because I like her. She tastes sweet."

Rachel could see the wheels begin to turn inside Danny's head. He looked at the dachshund sleeping at his feet. "I like Doxy," he said, a pensive expression on his face. "I wonder. . . ."

Becky, who'd been laughing at her sister's discomfiture, reached for her son. "No!" she said firmly. "People don't kiss dogs' ears."

"Not fair."

In spite of herself, Rachel laughed.

"Did you know I'm gonna have a birthday soon?" Danny, mollified now that he'd disturbed the dog's nap and put Doxy on his lap, turned to Scott. "Mom's gonna have a party for me. You can come."

"Uncle Scott probably has to work," Rachel said. She doubted he would want to be part of the pandemonium that characterized children's parties.

"Do you want me to bring anything?" Rachel asked her sister.

"Would you mind?" Becky's relief was obvious. "I was trying to think of some kind of dessert I could give the mothers. The kids will have ice cream and cake, but I wanted something different for the adults."

Rachel nodded. Canela boasted an excellent bakery, and she was sure Mary Jo, the woman who ran it, would have several suggestions.

It hadn't been her imagination, Rachel reflected half an hour later when the speeches were still droning on: The July 4th speeches *did* last forever. She was sure they'd have to wait for the seasons to change before the mayor, the police chief, the school superintendent, and half a dozen other dignitaries had finished presenting their views of patriotism.

"Too bad we don't have that hot air balloon here," Scott whispered. "We wouldn't need the propane."

Rachel laughed.

At last the speeches ended, and the crowd dispersed, spreading blankets under the trees or staking out spots at the picnic tables as they waited for the signal that the barbecue was ready. Preparations had begun the previous night, and by noon the aromas of spicy sauce and grilled meat made more than one mouth water in anticipation.

"You stay here with Dad and Uncle Scott," Becky admonished her son as she and Rachel rose to join the line. Though no one knew how it had started, Canela tradition said that the women waited in line and brought back food for their families.

Scott unfolded his long legs and stood next to Rachel. "C'mon, Tim," he said. "Let's get some grub. It's too hot for Rachel and Becky to stand in line."

Tim raised a brow and muttered something that sounded like "women's work," but Scott was undeterred. "Real men," he said firmly, "may not eat quiche, but they sure as blazes eat barbecue. And this is one man who thinks that if his wife faints, it ought to be for a better reason than standing in the sun."

He kissed Rachel soundly, then gave her a gentle push. "Sit down, sweetheart. If I learned anything in the Marines, it was how to wait in a chow line."

As the two men made their way toward the food, Becky turned to Rachel. "You sure found yourself a knight in shining armor, didn't you?"

Somehow Rachel managed a smile. On the surface, Scott was romance personified, every woman's dream of a husband. Surely there was no one in Canela who had the slightest inkling that their marriage was a lie, an empty shell. But how did he do it? How could he be so convincing in his role of pretend husband when it was Justine he loved?

"How was the celebration?"

Rachel was in Mary Thomas's room for her daily visit to Magnolia Gardens. Though Mrs. Nelson had told her the residents were content to receive weekly visits, Rachel's had quickly become daily. She told herself that Mary enjoyed her company, but the truth was, Rachel also enjoyed their time together.

In response to Mary's question, Rachel pulled out an envelope of snapshots she and Becky had taken. "This is my sister's family," she said.

"And who's the handsome man?" Mary studied each of the photos carefully, chuckling at the ones of Danny and Doxy, but when she finished, she held out a picture of Scott eating a plate of barbecue. It was Rachel's favorite shot on the roll. Somehow she had managed to capture Scott looking relaxed and totally happy.

"That's Scott. My husband." It still seemed strange to refer to him by that term.

"Quite a man," Mary said with a sweet smile. "You say he's from Canela, but I don't think I knew his family."

Rachel poured a glass of the lemonade she had brought for Mary and handed it to the older woman. "I'm not surprised that you didn't know them. There was only his mother. She moved here after her husband died and kept pretty much to herself."

"Grief will do that to a person." Mary nodded. "Your grandmother was devastated when her Jimmy died. We all worried about whether she might wish herself into the grave with him."

Rachel blinked in surprise. She knew that her grandfather's name was James and that he had died when he was in his late twenties, but beyond that, she knew very little of her grandmother's husband.

"Grandma never talked about him," she told Mary. "We didn't even have any pictures in the house." Rachel and Becky had thought that odd and had speculated that their grandparents' marriage had been a loveless one and that Laura had sought to forget it.

Mary took a sip of the lemonade, then nodded as though Rachel had confirmed something she suspected. "The pain was too great," she said. "You should have seen Laura and Jimmy together. When they were courting, they were inseparable, and once Laura's parents agreed they could marry, I don't think anyone had seen a couple so much in love. It almost hurt to see them together, because it reminded the rest of us that we were outsiders."

The picture was so different from Rachel's imaginings that for a moment she was speechless with the realization that there were many parts of her grandmother's life she and Becky had never even guessed. To cover her confusion, she walked to the window and fiddled with the blinds.

When she was once more composed, she returned to Mary's bedside. They chatted for a few minutes longer, looking through the pictures Rachel had brought, talking about the parade and the fireworks. When it was time for Rachel to leave, Mary laid a hand on hers.

"I hope you don't think I'm a meddling old woman, but something's been troubling me." She paused for a second, waiting until Rachel met her gaze. "Tell me, my child, are you happy?"

The question took Rachel unprepared. "Of course," she said quickly. Thank goodness she wasn't Pinocchio whose fibs were immediately apparent.

"I hope that's true." Mary gave Rachel a long, appraising look, almost as if she doubted her words. "If there's one thing I've learned, it's that life's too precious to waste a single minute. If you're unhappy with something, fix it."

But what if it was something that couldn't be fixed?

* * *

"Are you sure you don't mind going?" Rachel handed him the last of the cheerfully wrapped gifts. Mindful of her admonishment that this one was fragile, he placed it on the back seat.

"I told you it was okay." Scott waited on the passenger's side of the car so he could open the door for her. It wasn't simply that his mother had taught him to be chivalrous, although that had been the reason he had started opening doors for Rachel, he continued the practice because it amused him to watch her reaction. It was so obvious that her feminist side, which insisted she was perfectly capable of opening doors for herself, warred with her feminine side, which enjoyed being waited on.

"I know you said that." Rachel swung her long legs into the car, giving Scott a glimpse of shapely calves. She was wearing one of her long, swirly skirts today. Though Scott wished she had chosen the short denim one, he doubted she would change clothes to please him. She was in a good mood today, and he had no intention of ruining it with a frivolous request.

"An afternoon with a dozen four-year-old boys is beyond the call of duty," Rachel continued.

"We can call it hazardous combat." Scott turned the key in the ignition, enjoying the sound of the finely-tuned engine. At least Rachel hadn't protested when he suggested the Mustang needed a major tune-up. "That way I'll collect extra pay."

"You mean half a million isn't enough?" She sounded outraged. "You need more money to go to Danny's birthday party?"

"Actually, money wasn't the kind of payment I was

thinking about." He gave her lips a long appraising glance and enjoyed the blush that stained her cheeks. No doubt about it, it was fun teasing his wife.

His wife. Now, that was a thought. He'd better make another call to Justine tonight, just to keep everything on track.

"Man, am I glad to see you." Tim greeted Scott with a slap on the back when they arrived at the small house. Rachel ran inside to help her sister, leaving Scott to bring in Danny's gifts.

"You mean you've forgiven me for making you stand in the chow line?" he asked.

Tim balanced four boxes in his arms. "You still owe me for that, buddy, but you've gotta admit it was pretty funny how many other guys wound up in the line." Tim laughed at the memory. "If I were you, I'd be careful where I went around town for the next few weeks."

"Luke told me a dozen men came into the station to complain."

Tim gave him an appraising look. "Did they buy gas at the same time?"

Scott laughed. "You bet."

"Then the laugh's on them. C'mon. We've got work to do." Tim led the way to the backyard.

"Just what kind of work did you have in mind?" The more he got to know Rachel's brother-in-law, the better Scott liked him, but he hadn't counted on working this afternoon.

"You're my assistant chef," Tim told him. "We've got custody of the grill."

Between strategizing over charcoal technique, the two men watched the boys playing the games that

Becky and Rachel had organized. To Scott's surprise, most were rough tumbling games, and when Danny took his share of falls, neither Tim nor Becky seemed alarmed. Scott would have thought that, given the boy's precarious health, they would be more protective of him. Instead, it appeared that he was leading a completely normal life.

How different Danny's childhood was from Scott's own. Though he had had no physical ailments, his mother had tried to protect him from cuts and bruises, forbidding him to play with other children. He had never had a rough-and-tumble party like this.

As Scott watched, one of the boys slid into the corner of the picnic table, scraping his leg. Blood began to ooze, and the child whimpered, then started to cry.

"It'll be okay, Jake." Rachel knelt next to the crying child, giving him a quick hug. Then she pulled a handkerchief from her pocket and wiped the wound. Another foray into the pocket produced a Band-Aid. After she put the orange and green Band-Aid onto Jake's leg, she patted his arm. "Now you've got a warrior's badge," she told him. "You're special."

Jake grinned and scampered back to the others, loudly proclaiming his status as a warrior.

It was amazing. Anyone watching her would have thought she had years of experience with children, but Scott knew that was far from the truth. Rachel's life in Dallas included no children, and she had told him that she saw Danny only occasionally. Was it an inborn talent? Was Rachel one of those women who was born to be a mother?

What a stupid question! What difference did it make whether Rachel had one, ten, or no children? She wasn't going to have his babies, for their agreement was one of business.

Justine. *Remember you have Justine*, he admonished himself. But this afternoon that thought did nothing to stop his attraction to Rachel.

"It was a great party. Thanks for helping!" Becky pushed back a lock of hair as she and Rachel tossed paper plates into the garbage bags Tim had provided for clean-up. "I know this wasn't tops on your list of things to do on a Saturday afternoon."

"I had fun," Rachel said, retrieving a crumpled napkin from the ground. All things considered, the yard had survived the boys' assault well.

Becky stopped, fisted her hands on her hips, and stared at Rachel. "You sound surprised."

"Actually, I am. A year ago—who am I kidding? Three months ago—I couldn't imagine enjoying watching kids throw water balloons and play tag. But, yes, it was fun." And part of the fun, although she would never admit it, had been watching Scott join in the games.

"Your cheesecakes were a big hit." Becky reached for the plate that held the last two, handed one to Rachel and bit into the other. "I had forgotten all about them."

"So had I. Mary Thomas reminded me of them the first time I met her." Rachel had planned to buy the "grown up" dessert, but her talks with Mary had piqued her curiosity, and she decided that if Grandma Laura could bake cheesecake, so could she.

"Where'd you find the recipe?" Becky licked the crumbs from her fingers.

"Grandma had an old-fashioned file box filled with recipes. Knowing Grandma, you won't be surprised to learn that they were carefully filed alphabetically within subject."

"You mean there wasn't a Dewey Decimal number on it, too?"

"That sounds like her, doesn't it?" Rachel laughed. "Remind me to look at the back of the card."

"Becky said this was the best party Danny's ever had. Thanks for going with me." Rachel leaned back in the car seat, glad that the day had gone so well, equally glad that it was over. It would be good to get home and relax, away from the noise of a dozen four-year-olds' shouts.

Scott said nothing.

"Thanks, Scott. I really appreciate it."

Again, he made no response. Rachel turned to stare at the man who shared her house. His hands gripped the steering wheel, his eyes were fixed on the road. Those lips that frequently turned up in a smile, the lips that could wreak such havoc with her senses when they kissed her, were set in a straight line, an expression that said more clearly than words, *No Trespassing*.

Something was bothering Scott. Maybe he hated children's parties. That seemed unlikely, given the way he joined in the games. Still, Rachel knew Scott was a superb actor. Perhaps he was only acting when he played water tag with Danny's friends. Maybe the party reminded him of things from his childhood that he'd rather forget. Knowing Mrs. Sanders, that was a possibility. Whatever the cause, it seemed apparent that he was unwilling to discuss it.

They drove home in uncustomary silence. Scott unlocked the front door, tossed his Stetson onto the coat rack, then strode to the den. It was time for his call to Justine. But half an hour later when she heard no voices, not even the sound of the TV, coming from the den, Rachel started to worry. Scott did not sulk.

She walked to the den and looked in. Scott was seated in his favorite chair, but instead of reading a magazine or watching TV, he was staring into the distance, his expression as forbidding as it had been in the car.

"What's wrong?" she asked softly.

He turned to face her. "Nothing." Though his voice was toneless, telling her as clearly as his expression that he wasn't interested in conversation, Rachel wouldn't acknowledge the hint.

"Nothing?" She raised a brow and tried to keep her voice light. Perhaps she could cajole him out of whatever was causing this mood. "You're doing an awfully good imitation of someone with something wrong."

Scott shrugged. "I can't help it if you don't like the way I look."

"My, my, aren't we touchy tonight?"

His eyes opened wide, and for an instant she saw behind the defenses he had erected. The man was in pain, terrible pain.

"Just leave me alone, okay?" He sounded weary, and the sound made Rachel want to cry. She had always thought of Scott as invincible. Perhaps it was just the aura he wanted to project, a legacy of his years in the Marine Corps, but he seemed oblivious to pain.

Oh, she didn't doubt that he felt it, but she thought that he had been trained to overcome it.

"It's not something you can help with." Scott turned his back to Rachel, shutting her out with both words and actions, leaving her unsure which hurt more.

The problem was Justine. She knew that. It all came back to her and the intolerable situation they'd created.

If things were this painful now, how were they going to survive the rest of the year?

Chapter Nine

Rachel frowned as she poured her first cup of coffee. Though she knew caffeine solved no problems, it
might clear some of the fog from her brain. And then
maybe she would be able to make some sense of her
life. It seemed that Danny's party marked a turning
point in her marriage. Whereas previously Scott had
spent most evenings at home, now he was rarely in
the house. He would leave before Rachel woke, return
for a quick dinner, then go back to the station, where
he stayed until almost midnight.

When Rachel asked him why he was spending so
much time at the station, he answered that it was their
busiest season. That was true, but somehow his words
rang false. It appeared that Scott preferred to be at the
station rather than at home; what Rachel didn't know
was why, and that bothered her more than she wanted
to admit. She stayed awake each night until she heard
Scott return, and even after she knew he was safely
home, she slept fitfully.

"Aren't you the sleepy head?" Becky asked, eyeing

her sister's bathrobe. "You can tell you don't have children. You'd never be able to stay in bed this late. Maybe one day soon?"

Not for the world would she admit to her sister that her marriage was a sham, designed for one reason and one reason only: to ensure that Danny had his surgery. At first Rachel had wanted to tell Becky the truth, but now she couldn't—not without admitting that she had made the biggest mistake of her life. Living with Scott was a mistake, no doubt about it.

"I know there's a carton of toys in the attic," Becky said when she and Rachel had shared a pot of coffee. "I thought Danny could use a couple, so why don't I go look for them while you get dressed?"

Rachel nodded, glad that Becky wasn't going to follow her into her room. It would take some fast talking to explain why there were none of Scott's belongings in the room that she supposedly shared with him.

Fifteen minutes later, wearing an old pair of jeans and one of Scott's T-shirts, Rachel joined her sister. It felt odd slipping her arms into Scott's shirt, almost as though she were being enfolded in his embrace. She wouldn't have done it if he were home, but this morning she felt the need to convince her sister that hers was a real marriage.

"Look at this!" Becky held up a doll whose bridal gown had suffered from one too many pressings at the hand of a young girl. "Do you remember when Grandma gave me this? I was the envy of all my friends."

Though the gown was scorched and the hair needed expert attention, it was still a lovely doll.

Rachel touched the satin, remembering how thrilled

Becky had been that Christmas, finding the doll of her dreams beneath the tree. "I'm surprised that Grandma Laura would spend that much money on something as frivolous as a toy," Rachel admitted. "She seemed to begrudge every penny she spent on us."

Becky sat back on her heels and stared at her sister. "What do you mean? We never wanted for anything."

Rachel looked from the doll to Becky and shook her head. "How can you say that? We may have had material things, but Grandma always made sure we knew how much they cost." She clenched her fists, then—realizing what she was doing—forced herself to relax. She would not give her grandmother the satisfaction of annoying her from the grave.

Taking a deep breath, Rachel expelled it slowly, then said, "I used to think Grandma was born with a calculator in her hand. I'll bet she knew to the last penny just how much she spent on each of us every month." How that had rankled, that everything had a price.

But Becky, it appeared, hadn't minded. "She was teaching us values," Becky said. "Grandma wanted us to know that if we bought one thing, it meant we couldn't have something else."

Rachel couldn't help it. She threw up her hands in exasperation. "Ah, yes, the famous 'opportunity cost.' How many kids in Canela were lucky enough to be raised with a would-be economist?"

There was a moment of silence as Becky digested her words. To Rachel's surprise, her sister closed her eyes, and from the way her lips trembled, Rachel thought she was trying not to cry. It couldn't be. There was no reason to cry.

"Look, Rachel, I know you and Grandma didn't always get along," Becky said softly. Her voice was so calm that Rachel realized she was mistaken in thinking Becky was upset. As Rachel wrinkled her nose at her sister's gross understatement, Becky continued, "Okay, so you *never* got along. But you didn't understand her."

"I understand she didn't love us. That came through loud and clear." Rachel pulled a Slinky out of the toy box and began playing with it. Anything to hide the fact that her anger was still strong enough to make her hands tremble. "I can't tell you how shocked I was when Mary Thomas told me Grandma had been deeply in love with her husband. I wanted to ask her if we were talking about the same Laura Fleming."

"I knew she loved him."

"You did?" Rachel's hands stilled.

"Sure. When Tim and I were engaged, Grandma told me about her marriage and that she wished you and I would find the same happiness she did." Becky's smile was bittersweet. "Jimmy was the love of Grandma's life. That's why she never remarried."

Rachel still wasn't convinced. "Maybe that's why she didn't love us. She gave all the love she had to him."

Becky grabbed the Slinky from Rachel and threw it into the toy box. "Rachel, what's gotten into you?" she demanded. "Grandma loved us. Look at the way she took us in and raised us. Why would she do that if she didn't love us?"

"Duty." Rachel's answer was succinct. "I never said she didn't have a strong sense of duty. But love's something else."

The distinction was something Rachel knew all too well. She had married Scott without loving him, and look what that had gotten her. A sham of a marriage that became more difficult each day.

"Grandma Laura loved us," Becky repeated.

"And I suppose you're going to tell me she was heartbroken when I left town."

Becky nodded. "That hurt her badly. She wanted you to come home."

"Well, here I am."

"And now you're married to a wonderful man. Grandma would be so happy."

Someone ought to be.

"How should I know what dessert to bring?" Scott couldn't contain his annoyance. Since he had come home from work, it seemed that all he and Rachel did was snipe at each other. Now she wanted him to decide what kind of dessert to take to dinner. As if he cared! "Take a cake," he retorted.

She bowed low, her hand sweeping the floor. "As you wish, oh master."

For a second Scott was tempted to laugh, but he knew that would only fuel Rachel's anger. "Let me guess. You've been watching old sitcoms, and this is your best rendition of 'I Dream of Jeannie'."

"I've been giving the TV its daily exercise." Her voice held that acid tone he knew meant she was in a particularly bad mood. "That used to be your favorite pasttime. Now all you do is work."

If he didn't know better, Scott would have said that she missed him. Since he did know better, Scott figured something else had put her into a snit. In all likelihood, she was getting bored with her days at the nursing home and missed the excitement of Dallas. Unfortunately, there wasn't much he could do about that.

"Look, Rachel, I'm sorry if you don't approve, but that's the way I earn my living. I work."

"And because you stay at the station so late, you can call Justine from there."

He shrugged. Though she sounded jealous, that was about as unlikely as her missing him. "As you say, that's a fringe benefit."

She glared at him, her lips pursed in anger. "I don't want to go tonight."

"You've made that abundantly clear. Are you sure you don't want to take out a billboard, too?" When Rachel refused to answer, he continued. "You can't have it both ways, Rachel. You're the one who complains we never go out together; you say we need to keep up appearances. When Billy Ray called and invited us over for dinner, it seemed like the perfect opportunity."

Rachel fisted her hands on her hips. "You really think I want to spend an evening with the lovebirds of Canela High? Puh-leez. Thirteen years of marriage should have dampened their enthusiasm, but—in case you didn't notice—they couldn't keep their hands off each other at our wedding."

So that was the problem. Rachel was skittish about displays of affection.

"What's the matter, Rachel? Are you tired of our arrangement?"

"As a matter of fact, I am."

He shouldn't be surprised. For the past week, she'd

been acting like a gopher that had been chased out of its hole. He shouldn't be hurt. After all, he had no illusions when he entered into this arrangement. And yet it rankled, knowing that she found his company so distasteful.

"I don't care. You may be willing to call it quits, but I'm not."

They drove to the Fredericks' in silence. When they arrived, Susan whisked Rachel into the kitchen, leaving Scott alone with Billy Ray.

"You look like you could use a drink, old buddy," Billy Ray said handing him a coke. "Let me guess. You've been spending too much time at the station, and Rachel's pissed."

Scott turned and stared out the window. "Something like that." It was close enough to the truth.

"I heard you've been burning the midnight oil, but that business is good."

Rachel was right. There were no secrets in Canela. It had been too much to hope for that the grapevine wouldn't notice his late hours. Fortunately, they didn't know why he spent so much time at work. "I can't complain," he told Billy Ray. "Each month the balance sheet looks a little better."

"At least you're earning the money honestly."

Something in Billy Ray's tone made Scott turn around. "Who isn't?"

"I've been hearing rumblings about that law firm Rachel used to work for," Billy Ray said. "Some questions about ethics."

Scott emptied his glass and held it out for a refill. "That's the first I've heard. I met a couple of the partners at our wedding, and they seemed okay." Not that he had noticed much beyond the incredible beauty of the woman who had promised to love and cherish him, the same woman who less than an hour ago had declared her unhappiness with their bargain.

Billy Ray shrugged. "It's only rumor, but I heard they bribed witnesses and jurors. A friend in Dallas told me they're getting a reputation for doing anything to make sure they win their cases."

Scott's hackles rose at the thought of Rachel being associated with illegal dealings. "You're not suggesting Rachel had anything to do with that, are you?"

As Billy Ray slugged down the last of his drink, he shook his head. "Of course not. I just figure it's good Rachel's out of there."

"You and me both, buddy."

As she and Rachel placed platters of grilled steaks, baked sweet potatoes and corn on the cob in front of their husbands, Billy Ray's wife, Susan, said, "I can't tell you how great it is seeing you two again." She took the chair next to Billy Ray and kissed him.

A foolish grin lit Billy Ray's face. "Yeah," he agreed. "I never thought I'd see you two married. Susan and I always figured Rachel would wind up with Brad Stewart and you'd marry Becky."

Marry Becky. The thought had never occurred to him. He looked at Rachel. Though her face was pink, she laughed. Apparently she found the idea of him with her sister as amusing as he did.

"Isn't it amazing the way things work out?" she asked, and for once her question was devoid of sarcasm.

Susan nodded in apparent agreement. "It makes you want to believe in happy endings, doesn't it?"

"I don't know about you guys, but I don't want to think about endings," Scott said. "Now, happiness . . . that's another story." He stretched his hand out and caressed Rachel's cheek. It was softer than his old flannel shirt and a whole lot more agreeable to touch.

"See, Billy Ray, they're just like us."

She had thought the days dragged, but they seemed fast-paced compared to this past evening. Rachel didn't know what was worse, watching Susan and Billy Ray together or being so close to Scott that she could practically hear his heart beat. All she knew was that the evening had seemed endless. Billy Ray and Scott had carried the conversation, talking about their businesses and swapping fishing stories. It had been a revelation for Rachel, for she hadn't known that Scott fished.

Something was definitely wrong tonight. He had come home from the station in a bad mood, and it had only worsened. Now they were home, and Scott was once more ensconced in the den.

Rachel wandered through the house, trying to convince herself that she was sleepy, but failed. Finally she let herself out the back door and headed for the gazebo.

The night air was soft, with a light breeze stirring the leaves and a sliver of a moon illuminating the path. It was a night for lovers, a time for whispered promises and sighs of pleasure. But tonight, as every night, she was alone. It was worse—so much worse—than she had ever imagined possible. How was she going to continue the charade? And what would she do when the year was over?

Rachel sank into one of the cushioned chairs and leaned her head back, trying to find an answer to her questions. There were no answers.

The grass muffled his footsteps, and so the first sound she heard was the screen door's squeak. Scott stood in the doorway, his tall frame silhouetted against the lighter gray of the night sky.

"There's something I want to tell you," he said.

Rachel rose and started for the door. There was no longer any hope of finding peace in the gazebo. "Not tonight," she said softly, unwilling to argue with him. "I don't feel much like talking." Especially when everything they said turned into a confrontation.

She reached for the doorknob, intent on her escape, but Scott, it seemed, had other ideas. He put his hand on her arm.

"Then we won't talk."

As if he had all the time in the world, he drew her close to him, wrapping his arms around her, fitting her curves to the angles of his body.

"Scott." She started to protest. What was he doing? Had he sensed how lonely she was, how she craved companionship and love?

"Hush. No words."

And as if to silence her, he lowered his mouth to hers and drew her closer to him.

Her breathing quickened, and she could feel her pulse race, matching his. It was heaven, being held next to Scott. Suddenly nothing mattered except being held in his arms, breathing in the spicy scent that was

Scott's alone, tasting the sweetness of his mouth. This was what she missed. This was what she needed to make her life complete. In the space of a heartbeat, her loneliness disappeared.

Everything was perfect.

Chapter Ten

It was the stupidest thing she'd done in a long time, maybe ever. Rachel poured water into the coffeemaker and switched it on. With some luck, a cup of strong coffee would clear her head. She frowned, not certain which she needed more: luck or a clear head. She hadn't had much of either last night.

How could she have let Scott kiss her again? Let him kiss her? Who was she trying to kid? That had been no one-sided kiss. She'd been an active and willing participant. And to call it just a kiss was an understatement. It had been an embrace, the kind of embrace that moviemakers accompanied with their most romantic theme music.

It had been wonderful. Rachel pulled a loaf of bread out of the freezer and popped two slices into the toaster. As the smell of cinnamon and raisins filled the room, Rachel smiled. "Wonderful" was another understatement. Not one of the superlatives in her vocabulary was adequate to describe Scott's kisses. "Heavenly." That was the only adjective that came

121

close. Never before had Rachel experienced anything so beautiful.

That was the problem. Rachel had no right to enjoy Scott's kisses, no right to be in his arms, for he loved another woman and was promised to her. It had been a moment of moonlight madness, caused by emotion. Nothing more. And yet, Rachel couldn't dismiss her reaction so easily. She had never been a woman given to flights of fantasy or moments of temporary insanity. Until last night. Every sensible thought had disappeared.

Thank goodness Scott had the presence of mind to stop. When he ended the kiss, they walked back into the house together, hand-in-hand, and climbed the stairs together. He kissed her gently, then walked to his own room.

And so she had spent the night alone, tossing, turning, even shedding a few tears as she tried to convince herself that Scott was a gentleman.

The coffeemaker gurgled one last time, and Rachel reached for a mug. At last! Now she would get the caffeine she needed. She stared at the carafe, then blinked in disbelief. What a morning! Though she had carefully measured the water and placed the filter in the brew basket, she had forgotten to add the coffee.

Even banging the cabinet door didn't relieve her frustration.

She was having a bad morning. Scott frowned when he heard the cabinet door slam. Maybe she would feel better now, though he doubted it. He knew it would take more than a few loud noises to ease his own frustrations this morning. As it was, he was being extra careful as he shaved, lest his own rotten mood cause his hand to slip. The last thing he or Rachel needed was a trip to the emergency room.

Scott ran the washcloth over his face, removing traces of shaving cream. If only he could rinse away last night so easily. Kissing Rachel was the second stupidest thing he had ever done. The number one dumb move was agreeing to this whole scheme. A marriage of convenience! Talk about stupid! It all showed what price a person would pay for ambition.

If only . . . but it was too late for recriminations now. Scott grabbed the towel, frowning at his reflection. He should not have gone to the gazebo. He had known she was there, and if he had had a single brain in his head, he would have known what would happen. But his brain—at least the cautious part—had not been fully engaged, and so he had reacted like any normal male would to a woman as gorgeous as Rachel. He had lost control; he'd forgotten everything he'd promised himself; he'd forgotten Justine. It wouldn't happen again.

"Good morning." When he entered the kitchen, Rachel was seated at the table, a plate of toast and a cup of coffee in front of her. She nodded in response to his greeting, looking much the way he felt: as if she hadn't slept at all. It was his fault. Scott knew that, just as he knew there was nothing he could say to make her feel better. *Sorry, I was stupid. It won't happen again.* That wouldn't do much for her ego. *Sorry, but you're the most beautiful woman I've ever seen, and I couldn't stop kissing you.* Not much better. The smartest thing would be to pretend that nothing happened.

Scott poured himself a cup of coffee and took the seat opposite her. "I expect to be late tonight," he told her. When she made no answer other than a noncommittal nod, he continued. "Don't hold dinner for me. Luke and I'll grab a burger somewhere."

Rachel finished her coffee and rose to refill the mug. Her back was turned as she said, "I'll leave you a plate in the refrigerator. You can microwave it when you get home."

Her voice was level, as normal as Scott had ever heard it. Maybe he was wrong; maybe last night hadn't bothered her. Maybe the cupboard door had just happened to slam shut. And maybe pigs really did fly.

It was one of those perfect summer days that Rachel remembered from her childhood, days when the deep blue Texas sky seemed to stretch forever, broken only by a few puffy cumulus clouds. Rachel rolled down the window and let the breeze blow her hair as she drove to Becky's. For a few moments she was a carefree teenager again. For a few minutes she would forget that last night happened and that it meant so little to Scott that he hadn't even alluded to it. Instead, she would think about her sister.

Becky had surprised her by calling and suggesting Rachel come for lunch before she went to Magnolia Gardens. Though the sisters talked almost daily, they usually had lunch together only on Thursdays. Those were what Becky had named "sitter and sister days." Today was Wednesday. Though Becky had denied it, Rachel knew there must be a reason—an important reason—why her sister couldn't wait until tomorrow.

"Where's Danny?" Rachel asked when she joined

Becky on the patio. Though Doxy lazed in the shade, there was no sign of Becky's son.

"He's at the sitter's," Becky said. She kept her eyes on the ground, but the corners of her mouth twitched.

"So, what's wrong?" It wasn't like Becky to send Danny to the sitter twice in a week. She was adamant about raising her child herself and had told Rachel on numerous occasions how important shared mealtimes were.

"Nothing's wrong. I just knew Danny couldn't keep a secret."

"Secrets? What's going on here, Rebecca Barton?"

Doxy yawned as Becky rubbed her back. When the dog flopped onto her side, Becky raised her gaze to meet Rachel's. "I'm pregnant!"

Rachel could feel the blood drain from her face. "That's wonderful," she said. And it *was* wonderful news. She knew Becky and Tim wanted a second child, and now they were going to have one. Of course she was happy for them. There was no reason for her to be envious and just a little sad. After all, she hadn't felt that way the first time Becky had been pregnant. Then she had rejoiced wholeheartedly with her sister. But today was different. Today Rachel was filled with unidentified longings and the sense that the empty spaces deep within her would never disappear. It must be because she was tired. These odd feelings could have nothing to do with Scott.

But as she drove to the nursing home, Rachel tuned the radio to a rock station, turning the volume up in an attempt to clear her mind of its disturbing thoughts.

"Let's go into my office." Mrs. Nelson, Magnolia Gardens' administrator, met Rachel as she walked through the front door. "Would you like some coffee or iced tea?"

Rachel shook her head. Judging from Mrs. Nelson's expression, whatever she had to say wasn't pleasant.

"Did Mary fall again?" Her leg had been out of traction for a week, and though she was in a wheelchair, she had been walking a few steps every day.

Mrs. Nelson shook her head. "It's not that. Mary's taken a bad turn."

A bad turn. That could mean so many things. "What kind of bad turn?" Rachel gripped her shoulder bag to keep her fingers from trembling.

"She had chest pains last night. They're gone now, but they left her very weak." Though Mrs. Nelson's voice was calm, her expression told Rachel how grave the situation was.

"Should she be in the hospital?"

Mrs. Nelson shook her head again. "The doctor says it's not necessary, and Mary has refused to go."

Rachel steeled herself as she walked toward Mary Thomas's room, but even that didn't prepare her for the sight of the tiny woman lying in her bed, her face almost as pale as her white hair. She looked ten years older than the last time Rachel had seen her, only yesterday.

"Don't look like that, child." Mary's voice was strong, belying her fragile appearance. "I'm not dying yet." She clicked off the TV.

"Don't even talk about dying." Rachel pulled a chair close to the bed and took Mary's hand, holding it between both of hers. Surely it was only her imagination that Mary's hand felt colder than usual.

Mary shook her head slightly and smiled. "At my

age, death is something I think about a lot, but I'm not afraid of it."

"The doctor told Mrs. Nelson it was just a scare and that you'll be good as new soon." That was *not* what the administrator had said. This wasn't denial, Rachel told herself. It was positive thinking.

"What do doctors know?" Mary squeezed Rachel's hand, giving her the oddest feeling that Mary was comforting her, when it should have been the other way around. "The Good Lord has his ways of preparing us for new horizons. Now, child, put a smile on that pretty face of yours and tell me what you and that handsome husband of yours have been doing."

Rachel gave Mary a highly edited and fictionalized account of their dinner with Susan and Billy Ray. Ever since the day Mary had asked Rachel if she was unhappy, she had been careful to tell Mary only what she thought the woman would like to hear, amusing anecdotes and stories of Scott's romantic moments. Rachel hadn't had to invent the latter; all she had to do was make sure that Mary had no reason to suspect they were all for show and that their life together was far from idyllic.

The older woman had been enchanted with the tale of their one-month anniversary dinner, and she chuckled when she heard about Scott's attempts to surpass the lovebirds with sweeter words and more caresses than even Susan and Billy Ray could manage.

"The gazebo?" Mary's eyes sparkled, and Rachel wondered why she had told her about the kiss they had shared there. She hadn't meant to say anything about that. It had just slipped out. "Your grandmother would have been scandalized. Then again," Mary tipped her head to one side, reconsidering, "maybe not. Laura always had a twinkle in her eye when she talked about the gazebo. I wouldn't be surprised if she and Jimmy had their share of rendezvous there."

Rachel did not want to think about her grandmother, and she most definitely did not want to think about the gazebo. She should never have told Mary about last night.

"So, what else is new?" Mary asked. She leaned back on the pillows and closed her eyes, as though the effort of talking had tired her.

"My sister's pregnant again."

Mary opened her eyes and smiled at Rachel. "A new life. Wonderful! We'll have to make room for it."

As she drove home, Rachel wondered just what Mary meant.

Rachel must have left the light on for him. It was after midnight when Scott pulled in the driveway, and he was surprised by the extra light. He expected the front porch to be lit; Rachel always switched that on for him. But she had never before turned on the lamp in the den.

As he looked into the room, Scott stopped, startled. For not only was the lamp lit, but Rachel was there, sitting on the couch, staring into the distance.

"Rachel, honey, what's wrong?" As soon as the words were out of his mouth, Scott could have cursed. The endearment had just slipped out, and if Rachel's mood was anything like it had been this morning, she wouldn't appreciate being called "honey."

She turned, her face so filled with anguish that Scott realized she hadn't noticed his choice of words.

"Mary's ill. I think she's dying." Rachel's voice broke as she uttered the last word.

Scott crossed the room in two quick strides, then drew Rachel into his arms and held her close. Though he half-expected her to pull away, she didn't.

"Have you talked to Mary's doctor?" he asked, as alarmed by Rachel's trembling as he was by the news of her friend's illness.

"I tried," she said, and Scott saw tears well in her eyes. "They wouldn't tell me anything because I'm not family. Oh, Scott." Rachel buried her face in his shirt and began to sob. "Mary seems like family to me."

Scott held her close, handing her tissues and letting her cry. When the worst seemed to have passed, he said gently, "You've been her family, too." Though he had never put the thought into words, Scott suspected that Rachel saw Mary Thomas as a substitute for her own grandmother.

He kept his arm around Rachel, hoping she would take the comfort he offered. "Sweetheart, I'd like to tell you Mary's not going to die, but I can't. I'm not God. I can only tell you that you've brought her happiness, and that's all anyone can ask of each other."

Rachel raised her tear-stained face to his and managed a weak smile. "Thanks, Scott." She stared at him for a long moment, then to Scott's surprise, she pressed a kiss on his lips. "You're wonderful," she said.

Chapter Eleven

She hadn't remembered the traffic being so bad. In the thirteen years she had lived in Dallas, she commuted into the city each morning, complaining when the freeway traffic snarled and horns blared, but never letting it bother her. Today, though, it seemed heavier than usual even though it wasn't rush hour and she was riding in a taxi rather than driving her own car. Had she forgotten, or was it simply that there were no traffic jams in Canela?

Mary had nodded sagely when Rachel said she was going to Dallas for the day, insisting that although she would miss their visit, it was important that Rachel go. "It's time," she said. Seemingly recovered from her chest pains, Mary was back in her wheelchair, busy directing the other residents' activities.

As the taxi screeched to a stop in front of the building where she had worked for so many years, Rachel smiled. It was good to be back. For the past few days, she had been restless and nothing, not even her afternoons at the nursing home, had seemed right. She felt out of sync with Mary, Becky and, most of all, Scott. And so she had called her friend and former coworker, Megan, to arrange a lunch date.

"It's great to see you!" Megan hugged her and then stepped back, studying her.

Rachel wished she could say the same. Though Megan's smile was as warm as ever, there were new lines of strain on her face, and even her skilled application of makeup couldn't disguise the shadows under her eyes. In all the years Rachel had known Megan, she'd never seen her looking so haggard.

As the two women waited for an elevator to take them back to the lobby, Megan shifted her weight from one foot to the other in a nervous gesture that surprised Rachel.

"Is something wrong?" They had been friends for too long to mince words. Megan shook her head, apparently dismissing Rachel's question. "Nothing except that I lost the pool." She clenched and unclenched her hand.

Rachel raised one brow. For whatever reason, Megan didn't want to admit something was bothering her.

"Pool? What are you guys betting on now—the day Art finishes that 55-gallon drum of aspirin?" The managing partner's supply of painkillers was legendary.

As they stepped onto the elevator and she punched the lobby button with more force than necessary, Megan said, "Guess again. Closer to home this time."

When her next two guesses were wrong, Rachel held her hands up in defeat.

"The pool was how long it would take you to come back."

"Me?" Megan's words surprised her. Rachel had resigned from her job rather than taking a leave of absence because she wasn't sure she would be returning to the law firm when her year in Canela had ended. With the money she would inherit, she wouldn't have to work, at least not immediately. Perhaps she would spend a year traveling.

"Come on, Rachel." Megan's voice held more than a hint of mirth. "Canela's a cute little town, and you've got one hunk of a husband there, but it's not Dallas."

Megan had done nothing but vocalize Rachel's thoughts. There was no reason to be annoyed with her. Still, Rachel felt her hackles rise. It was one thing for her to disparage Canela, another for an outsider to do the same.

"Rachel!" As Rachel and Megan left the elevator, they met Art Langston, the partner who had been Rachel's primary boss. "When are you coming back?" he demanded. "Jessica's good, but she can't compare to you."

Rachel smiled. One of the reasons she had liked working for Art was that he wasn't afraid to praise his employees. "Jessica's outstanding, and you know it, but it's still nice to know you miss me."

"So, when are you coming back?"

Everyone, it appeared, assumed she would return. "Not for at least a year. I've got commitments in Canela."

Art nodded, then glanced at his watch as if reminded of his own immediate commitments. "Whenever you're ready, there'll be a spot for you. And if I can help you in the meantime, just call." He flashed Rachel a smile as the elevator closed, conveying his was not an empty offer. Art wasn't one to utter platitudes or politically correct phrases. He said what he meant, nothing more, nothing less.

When the waiter escorted Rachel and Megan to a table in the back of their favorite restaurant, and they ordered their ritual glasses of iced tea with lime, Megan turned to Rachel. "So, what do you do with your days? We've all been trying to figure out what you do with all that free time."

Rachel held out her hands, which were devoid of polish and had three ragged cuticles because the salon was closed for a two-week vacation. "As you can see, I have my nails done every day. After that, I sit by the pool and sip mint juleps. Or is it margaritas? I can never remember."

As she'd hoped, Megan laughed. "Okay. So I was prying. Now, tell me the truth."

Rachel waited until they ordered their salads before she answered. When she finished, she said quietly, "It's not quite like life here."

"No," Megan agreed with a wistful smile. "But I've got to admit that it sounds nice . . . at least for a while. And you look like you're thriving there."

There was a note in Megan's voice that raised Rachel's antennae. Though she might deny it, something was worrying her friend.

"How about you?" she asked, hoping to learn what was causing Megan's nervousness. "Are you still dating Sid?" If she'd broken up with her long-term boyfriend, that might explain things.

"Is the Pope Catholic?" Megan retorted. "Sid and I are a Dallas institution. We'll never break up, but we'll probably never get married, either. And, no, that's not bothering me."

Megan was silent for a moment, pushing a lettuce leaf around her plate with a level of concentration a brain surgeon might envy. She speared the lettuce, then laid the fork back on the plate.

"I guess there's no point in denying it. You always did see too much," she told Rachel. "The problem is that I'm worried about Sean." Sean was Megan's brother, the man Megan had once hoped Rachel would marry.

"What's he doing? Is he still in Virginia?"

Megan nodded. "He says his company is doing phenomenally well."

That sounded like Sean. Though Rachel had once accused him of having the Midas touch, he had insisted his success was due to a lot of hard work and only a little bit of luck.

"And you're worried because he's doing well?" That wasn't like Megan; she wasn't a worrier.

"It sounds silly, doesn't it? It's just that he's working too much. I keep telling him he needs to play a little—you know, smell the roses the way you do."

Was that what she did? Rachel wasn't sure she would describe her life in those terms.

An hour later she leaned back in the airplane seat and closed her eyes, thinking about the day. It had been good to see Megan again, but it had been strange, too. Though the camaraderie they'd always shared was there, somehow they didn't have as many things in common. There had been long awkward periods when they hadn't seemed to know what to say next, and that had never, ever happened before. It was almost as though they'd met after a separation of many years, not two months.

Her face somber, Rachel realized that her life and Megan's had started to move in different directions. Though they would always be friends, they might never again be close confidants. Rachel gripped the armrest, her white knuckles the only visible sign of how deeply that thought saddened her. For if there was one thing she knew, it was that she needed a friend, someone who would listen to her worries and share her joys. Megan and Becky had always filled that role, but—though she loved them both dearly—they were no longer enough. She needed someone else, someone who saw her differently.

As the plane began its descent to Canela's landing strip, Rachel smiled. She had a friend, someone who had already shared her worries, comforting her the day Mary had been so ill. Scott could be her friend.

The house was redolent of spices when Scott returned from the station that evening. He sniffed appreciatively, more than a little surprised that Rachel was making dinner. He expected her to either order in food or try his specialty: freezer cuisine. Instead, it smelled as though she was preparing jambalaya.

"Are you sure you didn't go to New Orleans today?" he asked as he lounged against the doorframe. "That smells like the real thing."

"It is the real thing. Rachel Fleming's special jambalaya."

Talk about the real thing! Though Rachel wore a red-and-white gingham apron, Scott saw that her legs were clad in a pair of jeans, and she had on one of

those white T-shirts that made her tan look spectacu-
lar. She could have posed for a Miss Texas poster.

Scott swallowed deeply. *Food. Think about food*, he
admonished himself. "Smells like fresh bread, too."

Rachel shrugged and lifted the lid on the soup ket-
tle. "Didn't I tell you I was an expert with the bread
machine?"

"Even a novice like me knows that it takes hours to
make both bread and jambalaya. How'd you manage
that?" Her plane was due in only half an hour ago, but
she looked—and the kitchen smelled—as if she'd
been home for hours.

Rachel dipped a spoon into the rich stew, tasted it,
then added a dash more cayenne. "I came back on an
earlier flight," she said.

Scott gave her an appraising glance. He wouldn't
have been surprised if she'd stayed for dinner with her
former colleagues. But coming back early? That did
surprise him.

"Not a good day?" he asked.

She was silent for a moment. "A sort of strange
one," she said at last.

Scott guessed that she wanted to say more, but
something was holding her back. "Strange in what
way? Did someone offer you a bribe or something?"
Ever since Billy Ray had mentioned that Rachel's old
firm was suspected of offering bribes, the thought had
nagged at Scott. He wanted to discuss it with Rachel,
but the time never seemed right. Tonight, though, she
had given him the opening he needed.

Rachel put the lid back on the jambalaya, then
looked at him, apparently puzzled. "What do you
mean?"

"Just that I've heard rumors that the firm bribes witnesses and jurors. I thought they might have made you an offer you couldn't refuse to return to work."

"Bribes!" Rachel's eyes widened in shock. Either she was a good actress, or this was the first she had heard of the dishonest dealings. "I can't believe that. Oh, I'm not going to deny that the partners and associates work hard looking for loopholes." Rachel tossed her potholder onto the counter and took a step toward Scott. "I've helped them do the research," she said. "We tried to find ways to win cases on technicalities. But dishonesty? That's not like them."

She sounded so convincing that Scott was reassured. After all, Rachel had first-hand experience with the firm. Billy Ray heard nothing more than rumors, and Scott had good reason to know that rumors frequently had no substance behind them. Look at the rumors about him and Rachel.

He took a step into the kitchen. "So, how was your day strange?" he asked.

Rachel laid place mats on the table, then opened the silverware drawer. "Was it Thomas Wolfe who said you can't go home again?" she asked. "That's how I felt."

"But you *are* home again."

Twin furrows appeared between Rachel's eyes as she considered his words. "I am, aren't I?"

The jambalaya was delicious. Scott wasn't sure if it was due to her disturbing day, the good food they shared, or something else, but Rachel seemed different tonight: softer, mellower, and, if it were possible, more beautiful. They both took second helpings of the spicy stew, washing it down with glasses of iced tea. Although Rachel offered him beer, Scott demurred, saying he had to go back to the station. But as he helped her clear the dishes, he found himself unwilling to leave. There was nothing so urgent that it couldn't wait until the morning. And so he went into the den once they finished loading the dishwasher.

Rachel followed him into the room, taking a seat in the rocking chair across from him.

"When we were kids, did you ever think we'd wind up here together?" she asked.

What a question! Talk about opening Pandora's box. No matter how he answered, he would stir up trouble.

"Not even in my wildest dreams did I think we'd be here," he said, with a slight emphasis on the last word. That was the truth, the literal truth. If it wasn't the complete truth, only Scott needed to know that.

"Me neither." Rachel leaned her head back and began to rock slowly. "I'm still surprised, though, that you came back to Canela."

Scott could feel himself relax. This was a less dangerous subject. "Houston was great," he admitted. He had enjoyed many aspects of living in the city. "But I found that I liked small towns better."

Rachel nodded, and, maybe it was only Scott's imagination, but she seemed more relaxed. "My grandmother used to say they were the real America."

"She was quite a woman. All of us kids used to be afraid of her."

"You should have lived with her." Rachel's voice held irony, not bitterness, and Scott realized this was the first time he had heard her speak of her grandmother without rancor.

"No, thanks." Scott chuckled. "My mother was enough."

Rachel stopped rocking and leaned forward, her hands on her knees. "Your mother and my grandmother were so different they seemed like different species, not just two different generations."

"You're probably right about that." Scott studied his boots as if they could tell him why he and Rachel were having this conversation. "Different" was the right adjective, though he would have applied it to Rachel rather than his mother or her grandmother. But Scott knew better than to vocalize his thoughts. Instead, he said, "All I knew was how much I resented Ma's attention. There were times when I thought she was going to smother me. It took a long time before I realized that everything she did, she did out of love."

Rachel was silent for a moment, and he could tell from the way she fidgeted that she wasn't comfortable with the subject of love. "Becky and Mary keep telling me the same thing, that my grandmother loved us," she said at last. "I guess I'm a few steps behind you, because I still don't believe it."

"Don't think that I'm happy about the way Ma raised me. I didn't say that; I just said that I've learned to accept it." Scott watched the tiny frown lines between Rachel's eyes begin to disappear. "One thing I learned in the Marines is that you've got to take responsibility for your life. Change what you can. Accept the rest."

"But don't you have some regrets?" Rachel's tone made it clear that she had more than one.

"Sure. Mostly I'm sorry that I didn't have a normal

life as a teenager. There were so many things Ma wouldn't let me do."

"I know the feeling."

Rachel rose, asking Scott if she could bring him a drink, and he guessed she wanted a change of subject as much as a cold drink. When she returned from the kitchen, she placed a bowl of pretzels on the table between them and started talking about the latest movie.

The bowl of pretzels was empty, and Scott had refilled their glasses, when he noticed Rachel stifling a yawn. He glanced at his watch, then looked at it again, surprised.

"It's midnight," he said. "I didn't realize it was so late." In truth, he hadn't thought about the time. It had been so enjoyable talking to Rachel—really talking to her—that he hadn't considered how long they'd been in the den.

She smiled. "This was the best evening I've had in a long time." And she sounded as though she meant it.

Rachel stared at her reflection, then frowned. She'd done it again. Though it had been only ten minutes, she had gnawed off her lipstick. At this rate, she would need a new tube before Scott got home.

It was silly to be so nervous. It wasn't as though Scott was a stranger, and he certainly hadn't complained when she told him of her plans. Oh, he wanted to know the details, but she hadn't been willing to divulge them. Surprises, she told him, were good. All he needed to know was that they were going on a date.

"A date? Why?"

"Why not?" Rachel wasn't going to admit that this was part of her plan to turn Scott into her best friend. "I thought we both agreed that we needed to be seen in public." Of course, her plans didn't include a lot of public appearances, but Scott didn't need to know that. Nor did he need to know the real reason why she had arranged this particular evening.

"Is this casual enough?" Scott asked when he appeared in faded jeans, his favorite cowboy boots and the black T-shirt Rachel had worn the day she and Becky had searched the attic for toys.

"Perfect." She'd chosen a short skirt and a scooped neck tee shirt, pulling her hair back into a high ponytail.

Though Scott raised an eyebrow, he didn't complain when she climbed into the driver's seat. "After all, I'm the one who asked you on the date," she reminded him.

"Then you're paying for dinner," he retorted.

"Of course." She pushed the cassette into the slot and watched Scott's mouth turn into a smile; she'd chosen the same high school hits that he had played the day after their wedding.

As she pulled the Mustang into one of the drive-up windows at the Sonic, Scott laughed. "Big spender, aren't you?"

She merely smiled and ordered hamburgers, fries and shakes for them.

"Is this your idea of five fruit and vegetable servings a day?" he demanded, reminding her of her efforts to change his eating habits.

"What do you mean?" Rachel pretended to be outraged. "There's lettuce and a pickle on the burgers, and I have it on very good authority that potatoes are vegetables."

"Next thing I know, you'll be telling me that catsup is a vegetable."

"Now that you mention it . . . actually, I was going to point out that this is a date. You don't have to worry about the food pyramid on a date."

"Then let's make dinner a date every night."

"Are you complaining about my cooking?"

Scott patted his stomach. "Hardly. I've never eaten so well. But you have to admit that this is a little out of character." He took a big bite of the hamburger, making a show out of savoring its flavor. "Wait a minute. I'm starting to see a pattern. The old songs. The burger joint. What's next—a drive-in movie?"

"Precisely!" Rachel grinned. "I figured we ought to see what we missed as teenagers." She hoped, oh, how she hoped, that he would like the idea. Though he may not have realized it, his voice had been wistful when he told her about missing a normal teenage life. There was nothing Rachel could do to change that, but for one night, they could pretend they were both teenagers again.

They pulled into the drive-in and secured the speaker to the car's window. Scott pushed the seat back as far as it would go, stretching his legs out in front of him. "The younger generation has it easier," he announced. "You don't see them here. I'll bet they're all at home, watching videos on some comfortable couch."

"Stop complaining." Rachel knew Scott was merely grousing, but she couldn't resist teasing him. "Don't you know you're supposed to be polite on a date?"

"Even when my date takes me to a horror movie?" he asked.

"Do you have any idea how hard it was just to find a drive-in? They must be on the endangered species list. Now, do you want your popcorn with butter or extra butter?"

Scott merely laughed. "Healthy eating, huh?" he asked when Rachel handed him two chocolate bars, a Coke, and a box of popcorn.

"Nostalgia," she corrected him. "Did you count fat grams when you were a teenager?"

"No," he admitted. "In fact, I still don't."

And it was obvious that he had no need to. While the men she knew in Dallas had frequented gyms and health clubs, Scott had once told her he had no interest in planned exercise. Working at the station provided all the cardiovascular exercise and muscle toning he needed.

"Then just enjoy it," she suggested.

Scott munched a handful of popcorn as the movie's soundtrack began to squawk. "You know, Rachel," he drawled, "if we really were teenagers, we'd be in the backseat."

His words evoked images that Rachel found oddly disconcerting. The car was small; the backseat would be cramped. And yet . . .

"On a first date?" She raised an eyebrow. "I don't think so."

"I would have tried."

"And I'd have said 'no.' "

"Can't blame a guy for trying."

Scott leaned back in the seat, draping his left arm over Rachel's seat. Though he wasn't touching her, his arm was so close that she could feel its warmth on her neck, and when his fingers drummed on the head-rest, the vibration felt like a soft massage.

"Look at that!" Scott pointed toward the huge screen, then started to laugh. "That's the strangest monster I've ever seen." Though the creature's neck was scaly, his feet were covered with matted fur that reminded Rachel of a pair of bunny slippers she had as a child. Years after she'd outgrown them, she had kept them in her closet, where they'd gathered dust, then been chewed by a puppy Becky had smuggled in.

"I know his feet had scales in the last scene," Rachel said.

"If we rented the video, we could replay it."

"You and your videos! I keep telling you it isn't the same."

"You're right. I'd have kept my finger on the fast-forward button."

"Spoilsport."

"Hey, look at that!" As Scott continued his com-mentary, Rachel started to laugh.

"I don't think it was meant to be a comedy," she said when the final credits began to roll.

"With acting that bad, what else could you call it?" Scott chuckled. "One thing's for sure, if I ever decide to sell the station, I could get a job in Hollywood. I could do as well as those actors."

"Better." After all the practice he had pretending to be a happy husband, starring in a B movie would be simple.

They joked as they drove back to Canela, each try-ing to outdo the other in remembering amusing parts of the movie. Though it was certain "Return of the Green-Scaled Monster" would never win an Academy Award, Rachel couldn't remember when she had enjoyed a movie more.

When she parked the Mustang, Scott opened her door and said, "I think this is where I'm supposed to thank you for a nice evening."

Rachel smiled, remembering the times she had told that to dates but meant the exact opposite: that she never wanted to see them again. Although Scott had appeared to enjoy their pretend date, she couldn't be sure. After all, wasn't she the one who had noted how convincing he could be when he played a role?

"I'll spare you the polite words," she told him.

"No fair, Rachel. You said this was a date, and we're gonna play it all the way." He bent his head as though he were a shy teenager and said, "Thank you for a very nice evening."

"I'm glad you enjoyed it." Rachel murmured the correct words, hoping that Scott meant it. She had planned the evening for him, hoping he would take pleasure from doing the things he had missed during high school.

As she continued walking toward the house, Scott reached for her hand. "Aren't you forgetting something?" he asked.

"What?"

"You asked me on the date," he explained. "If this were a real date, you'd try to kiss me goodnight."

She stopped, surprised and yet tempted by his words. After the last time she and Scott had kissed, she had sworn she would never again give into the desire to kiss him. And, oh, the desire was strong. But it was wrong, so wrong, for he belonged to Justine.

"Well?" Scott stood motionless, waiting for her to make a move.

Rachel looked at him a moment longer, trying to decide. Why not? It was all part of a game, wasn't it?

She moved closer to Scott, putting her hands on his shoulders, tilting her head from side to side as though she were trying to figure out where their noses ought to go. Finally, she leaned forward and pressed a quick kiss on his lips.

As she started to move, Scott wrapped his arms around her, drawing her ever closer to him, molding his lips to hers. For a moment, Rachel thought of nothing beyond the joy of being held in Scott's arms. And then she remembered.

Justine.

Rachel backed away from him.

"That was quite a first kiss," she said, trying to keep her voice light, hoping it didn't betray her confusion. It had been a wonderful kiss. If only there was no Justine.

But there was.

Chapter Twelve

It shouldn't have felt so strange. Rachel doubted that anyone in Canela—even the people who spent their days searching for tidbits of gossip—would find it remarkable. Still, as she closed the lid of the picnic basket and lugged the surprisingly heavy container toward the gas station, she hesitated. How would Scott react? She had thought it would be a pleasant surprise. Now she wasn't so certain.

"Rachel!" Luke's eyes widened in surprise as she walked into the station. He sat in one of the two metal chairs, his feet propped on the other. "Is something wrong?" Boot heels hit the floor as he jumped to his feet.

Rachel suppressed a smile. It appeared she'd been right about the surprise part. The jury was still out on the "pleasant" verdict.

She shook her head in response to Luke's question and gestured toward the basket she had set on the floor. "I brought my husband lunch," she explained, looking around the room. Where was he? Scott hadn't been at the pumps, and his small office was dark.

"Lunch!" Luke sniffed appreciatively, then gave the basket a calculating look. "How do you feel about divorce?" he asked.

For a second Rachel's breathing stopped. Was this Luke's way of telling her that Scott wouldn't appreciate her bringing him lunch, that he didn't want to be bothered at the station?

"What do you mean?"

Luke grinned and reached for the basket. "I have to admit that I'm tempted. If I hadn't sworn off marriage, you can bet next month's paycheck that I'd try to talk you into leaving Scott." Luke made a show of salivating. "Those old ties that bind might not be so bad if they're tied to lunches."

He was joking. That was all. There was no reason for the sick feeling that had settled in the pit of her stomach at the thought of divorce. Rachel took a deep breath. "There's plenty for you," she told Luke, opening the lid to display both the quantity of food she had prepared and the three plates and glasses.

"I'm in love!"

"Who's the lucky girl?" Scott emerged from the garage, wiping his hands on a paper towel. The streak of grease on his cheek and the oil stain on his coveralls told Rachel he had just finished an oil change and lube.

"Your wife." Luke put a playful arm around Rachel's shoulders. As Scott frowned, Luke dropped his arm. "Only kidding, man. You know that." He moved back two steps. "Still, that fried chicken your wife brought for lunch smells good enough to make a man forget his principles."

Scott grinned and picked up the basket. "Rachel's cooking can do that. You should taste her jambalaya."

"Cruel!" Luke clapped Scott on the back. "You had jambalaya and didn't tell me! And to think you used to be my friend."

The three of them moved toward Scott's office. He switched on the light, then stood aside so Rachel could precede him.

"What about me?" Rachel demanded of Luke. "I thought Scott loved me for my mind."

"Your mind is only part of the package, darlin'," he drawled.

Rachel blushed, and Luke moved toward the door. "I can tell when I'm not wanted. Just give me some of that chicken, and I'll leave you two lovebirds alone."

"Sounds like a plan to me." Scott opened the basket. As Rachel started to dish out potato salad, biscuits and the chicken that piqued Luke's interest, Scott put his arm around her waist.

"Is today a special occasion?" Scott asked when Luke had closed the door behind him. "Did I forget something?"

"No and yes." When Scott looked puzzled, she continued, "It's not a special occasion, but you did forget to eat breakfast. I wanted to make sure you had lunch."

"And more of the famous fruit and vegetable servings." He looked at the plate of food Rachel had put in front of him, as though assessing its nutritional content.

"Someone's got to keep you healthy," she retorted.

Scott took a large bite of the chicken and murmured appreciatively.

The telephone's ringing interrupted the moment.

Scott shook his head. "Luke'll get it. If not, there's a machine." The third ring ended abruptly. "See?" He took another bite of chicken.

But a moment later, Luke knocked on the door. "Sorry to interrupt," he said as he poked his head into the room. "It's those guys from the agency. They've got more questions about one of the permits."

Scott muttered something under his breath, then reached for the phone. "Sorry, sweetheart," he said, his body language telling Rachel he wanted to be alone with his caller. "I'll be awhile." He pressed a quick kiss on her lips. "Leave the basket. I'll bring it home tonight."

"And it'll be empty," Luke promised as he and Rachel walked toward her car. The midday sun sizzled, and Rachel's sneakers stuck to the soft asphalt. She was glad she parked under the oak tree.

"I'll bet you'll be as happy as Scott when those permits are approved," Luke said as he opened the car door. "They sure turned into a hassle."

Rachel nodded. Not for anything in the world would she tell Luke that she had no idea what he was talking about. It was obvious the permits were important, and Rachel assumed they were related to Scott's plans for expansion, but—for all she knew—they could be permits to march in the Labor Day parade. She frowned and turned the key in the ignition.

"So, what's up?" Rachel asked ten minutes later when her sister answered the phone. Becky had left a message on the answering machine, telling Rachel to call the instant she got home. "Has Doxy had the puppies?"

Becky laughed. "Not yet. The vet says another week or ten days. No, Rachel, this is even better." Rachel heard a lightness in Becky's voice that hadn't been there in months, maybe even years.

"Danny," she said softly.

Rachel pulled out a chair and sank into it. Though Becky's happy tone must mean good news, her legs had suddenly turned to rubber.

"The surgery's scheduled for Wednesday," Becky said, and her voice, though shaky, reflected her joy. "Dr. Kingsley examined him today, and we had a conference call with Dr. Martin. She's the surgeon in Dallas," Becky explained. "They both think he's ready."

"That's wonderful!" Rachel wished she were in the same room as her sister. She'd throw her arms around her and dance a celebratory jig they way they had as children the day school ended. But this was much, much more important than a summer recess.

When Becky explained that surgery had been scheduled for eight A.M. and that it was expected to last five-to-six hours, Rachel said, "I'll be there." Though Becky and Tim were driving to Dallas the preceding day since Danny needed to spend the night in the hospital, Rachel could take an early flight and still be there before Danny was wheeled into the operating room.

Becky murmured her pleasure. "I was hoping you and Scott could be there. Tim and I are gonna need all the help we can get."

Scott. It still seemed strange to realize that Becky and everyone else in Canela considered him part of the family. They didn't know just how temporary the seemingly perfect marriage would be.

"I'll talk to him tonight," she said. "I'm sure Luke can manage the station for a day."

"That would be great. But if he's got a meeting about those permits or something, we'll understand. I know how worried Scott is about them."

Those permits again. They had something to do with the station; that much was obvious. And that meant it was logical that Luke would know about them. As for her sister, in all likelihood, Scott had mentioned something to Tim the last time they had dinner together, and Tim had told Becky. It wasn't as though there were a conspiracy of silence, a deliberate plan to keep Rachel ignorant. Scott had just forgotten to tell her. That was all. No big deal. There was no reason for her to feel so hurt, so excluded.

"You look worried," Mary said later that afternoon when Rachel handed her a piece of peach pie. She knew the older woman had a sweet tooth and had made a habit of bringing Mary dessert at least once a week. "Is it your friend in Dallas?"

Rachel shook her head, realizing she hadn't talked to Megan in days. "No," she said slowly, suddenly wanting to confide in someone. "This may sound odd, but I'm worried about Scott."

"The permits." Mary nodded, her expression solemn. She reached for her remote control and turned off the radio. Though she kept her voice low, Rachel had no trouble hearing every word. "I heard the EPA was being stricter than usual this time and that there was a good chance the expansion wouldn't be approved," Mary said. She studied Rachel's face, as if trying to read her thoughts. "I wondered if the story was true or the usual exaggeration, but I didn't want to pry." She laid her hand on one of Rachel's. "I figured that if you didn't want to talk about it, it's because you and Scott were too worried."

If only that were the case! Rachel closed her eyes for

a second, trying to marshal her emotions. She couldn't let Mary see how hurt and, yes, how angry she was.

At last she opened her eyes and faced Mary. "I didn't want to worry you," Rachel lied.

Mary was silent for a moment, and Rachel had the sinking feeling that her friend saw through her lies. "So, what's the story with Danny's surgery?" Mary asked when the silence became oppressive.

Relieved by the change of subject, Rachel smiled. "Are you a mind reader? Becky just called today with the good news."

But even though she kept a smile fixed on her face, Rachel could not quiet the anger that had begun to simmer. By the time Scott arrived home, it had reached the boiling point. Though she had tried to convince herself that Scott had not been hiding things from her, she hadn't succeeded.

"Did you do it deliberately?" she demanded as he walked into the kitchen.

Scott stared at her as though she'd suddenly started speaking a foreign language. "What are you talking about?" He placed the picnic basket on the counter next to the sink and began transferring dishes from it into the dishwasher as calmly as if nothing were wrong.

How could he? First he excluded her and now he was pretending to be innocent.

"Stop that!" Rachel's voice rose ten decibels. "I want an answer. Did you do it deliberately?"

Scott closed the dishwasher and turned to face Rachel, his expression guileless and a little perplexed. "Did I do what?" he repeated.

"Humiliate me. Make me the last to know."

Shaking his head as though to clear it, Scott spoke

slowly. "Rachel, I don't have a clue what you're talking about. You're obviously upset, but I can't help you if I don't know what's wrong."

The man was infuriating, absolutely, positively infuriating. "You're what's wrong," she said. "You and those permits. Everywhere I turn I hear about them. It seems like everyone in Canela knows about them except for me." She clenched her fists then released them. "Why should I know anything? I'm only your wife."

Scott was silent for a moment, his expression inscrutable. "I didn't know you were interested," he said at last. "To be honest, I got the idea that the subject was taboo." When Rachel raised an eyebrow, questioning his words, he continued. "What was I supposed to think? In all the time we've been married, you never asked about the station. You knew I was looking for investors, and you made it pretty clear that you didn't like that idea, but you never asked what had happened after we had dinner with the Wainscotts."

When Rachel started to speak, Scott held up a hand. "Hear me out. I spend half my waking time at the station, but until today, you never even drove by. Tell me, Rachel, why would I think you'd care that the EPA is hassling me over my storage tanks or that, with a stroke of his pen, some cursed desk jockey might destroy my plans for the expansion? You think I humiliated you. Turn it around, Rachel. How do you think I felt?"

Rachel had no answer.

Chapter Thirteen

She couldn't carry a tune, but it didn't matter. There was no one to hear her singing as she drove to Magnolia Gardens. The day was dismal, cloudy and damp, and the weatherman had predicted rain before dusk. Normally Rachel hated days like this, but today, even the less-than-perfect weather couldn't ruin her happiness.

It had taken so little—just one phone call—to help Scott. As soon as the office opened, she had called Art Langston, her former boss, and had asked him to pull whatever strings he could to ensure that Scott's permits were approved. As she expected, Art agreed, although he cautioned her that it might take several weeks, since his contacts at the agency might be on vacation. Still, he thought it highly likely that he would be able to help. Within two or three weeks, Scott should have his permits, and then nothing would stop his dream of expanding the station.

Dreams, as Rachel knew all too well, rarely came true. But this one would. She would make sure of that.

Scott was right. She hadn't done her part in making their arrangement a success. She hadn't considered his pride and how important appearances were. Though there was no way to undo the past, she could ensure that the future was better, and her first step was to do everything she could to get those pesky permits approved.

"Is everything ready for Danny's surgery?" Mary was seated in her wheelchair, gazing out the window when Rachel arrived. She turned at the sound of Rachel's footsteps and smiled.

Rachel nodded. "Becky and Tim drove him to Dallas today. Scott and I are going tomorrow morning." There was a conveniently scheduled commuter flight, but if there hadn't been one, Rachel would have chartered a plane. Nothing was going to keep her from Danny's bedside.

Mary leaned her head against the seat back and closed her eyes as if she were tired. She took a deep breath, then opened her eyes again. It was surely Rachel's imagination that those blue eyes looked clouded. "That nephew of yours is the spitting image of your grandmother," Mary said.

Rachel could feel her jaw drop. "Danny?"

"Do you have another nephew?" Mary asked dryly. When Rachel shook her head, Mary continued. "It's not so obvious in the pictures, but in person . . . his smile, the way he holds his head—he's a young, male version of Laura."

Rachel wasn't sure what surprised her more, Mary's assertion of Danny's resemblance to her grandmother or the fact that the boy had obviously come to the nursing home. Becky had said nothing of the visit.

"You saw Danny?" The question was unnecessary.

Mary nodded, and her eyes sparkled again. "Your sister brought him here yesterday. She said he wanted to see Aunt Rachel's old friend." Mary wrinkled her nose, then chuckled. "I ought to take offense at the description, but how can I dispute my age? It's what we used to call an incontrovertible fact."

"You're not old." Though Rachel knew Mary's biological age, to her the woman had never seemed old. Ageless was a better adjective. When they had discussed it in the past, Mary had told Rachel she enjoyed her status as an antique. "I worked hard to get here," she always said with a twinkle in her eyes.

But today, Mary's response was different. "Yes, child, I am old," she said firmly. "Old and very tired. Now, help me onto my bed."

The request surprised Rachel. Never before had she known Mary to take an afternoon nap, although many of the residents did. Still, there was no denying that today she did indeed look tired. Perhaps she had had a restless night.

When Mary was stretched out on the bed, the handmade quilt she had brought from home pulled to her waist, she turned to Rachel. "Will you humor an old woman?" she asked. "Hold my hand until I fall asleep."

"Of course." Rachel took her hand between both of hers and smoothed the wrinkled skin as Mary closed her eyes. When her breathing became the slow, even inspirations of sleep, Rachel rose. She reached the door and was closing it behind her when she turned once more. In two quick steps, she was beside Mary's bed. Bending down, she pressed a kiss on the older woman's forehead.

"Sleep well," she murmured as she left the room.

"I'm so happy you're here!" Becky was pacing the floor of the waiting room when Rachel and Scott arrived at the hospital the next morning. "Danny's kicking up a fuss. He told the nurses he won't go into surgery without seeing you."

Though the flight had been on time, there had been more traffic than usual, delaying their arrival at the hospital. Rachel had told herself that she was prepared, that Danny had the finest surgeons money could provide, but there was no denying her nervousness. Her hands trembled, and she found it difficult to concentrate on anything other than the upcoming surgery. As if sensing her fears, Scott held her hand in the taxi, and now as they walked through the hospital corridors, he kept his arm around her waist. In the past she might have thought the gesture was for show, part of Scott's "convince the lawyers" strategy, but today, Rachel knew Scott was doing everything for her, trying his best to comfort her.

"Can we go in?" he asked Tim when they reached Danny's room.

"You'd better." Tim managed a grin. "That son of mine is one stubborn boy. Must have gotten it from his mother's side of the family."

When Rachel refused to take the bait, Scott spoke. "Sure thing." He increased the pressure on Rachel's waist, propelling her through the door.

Danny lay there, looking pale and far too small to be enduring major surgery. The lump that lodged in

Rachel's throat prevented her from speaking, so she bent down and kissed him, while Scott held out his hand for the shake that was part of his ritual with Danny.

"What's this?" Scott asked, pointing to what appeared to be a miniature dog bone laying on the bedside table.

Danny grinned. "Mrs. Mary gave it to me. It's for the puppies, you know." His tone was conspiratorial, as though the puppies were a secret that only he and Mary Thomas knew but which he was willing to share with Scott and Rachel.

"I'm sure they'll like it." Rachel found her voice. If Danny could act as if this were an ordinary day, surely she could, too.

"Did you see the puppies?" he asked.

Rachel shook her head. "They aren't born yet. But they'll be there when you come home." Rachel had stopped at Becky's house that morning to feed Doxy, and unless she was mistaken, the dog's unusual restlessness was a signal that she was close to whelping.

"Okay, Danny." Two orderlies entered the room. "Are you ready now?"

Becky and Tim walked on one side of the gurney with Rachel and Scott on the other as the orderlies wheeled Danny to the operating room. All four kept smiles on their faces as they kissed Danny or—in Scott's case—shook his hand. But once the door was closed, Becky burst into tears.

"I'm so scared," she cried, burying her face in Tim's shoulder.

Tim stroked her hair. "He'll be okay."

Taking Rachel's hand in his, Scott led the way to

the waiting room. When he'd persuaded the other couple to sit on one of the faux leather couches, he said, "Danny's in God's hands now . . . and Dr. Martin's." He paused for a moment, then added, "I wouldn't worry if I were you. The doc looked like she could do almost as good a valve job as Luke."

His words broke the strain, and everyone laughed. "That's the ultimate compliment," Rachel said, as she wiped her eyes.

For the next six hours, they alternated between pacing the floor, staring sightlessly at the television, attempting to play Monopoly and drinking countless cups of bitter coffee. Though they tried valiantly to pretend otherwise, their thoughts held only one object: the small boy whose future was being decided behind the beige doors. And yet, throughout the day, Scott tried to interject humor, to find small things that would distract them, if only for a moment. Each time he did, Rachel smiled, realizing how much Scott was doing to make the day more bearable. What would they have done without him?

At last the doors opened, and the surgeon approached Tim and Becky. Though Dr. Martin still wore her surgical gown, she had discarded her mask, revealing the lines of strain on her face. But as Tim and Becky hurried toward her, trailed by Rachel and Scott, she smiled.

"Success!" she said. "Your son's in the ICU, and you won't be able to see him for a couple hours, but he's fine. The surgery was perfect."

A second doctor joined Dr. Martin. Though he too was in scrubs, his face was more relaxed than the surgeon's. "We should have videotaped this. It was a textbook example of great surgery."

Rachel doubted her sister heard anything beyond the doctor's declaration of success, for Becky turned to Tim, hurling herself into his arms, crying tears of pure happiness.

He was going to be okay! Her precious nephew would have a normal childhood! Rachel turned to Scott, and when he opened his arms, it felt natural to move into them, to take comfort from the strength of his embrace, the softness of his lips on her forehead.

Scott and Rachel stayed at the hospital until Tim and Becky were able to see Danny. Then they left for the airport. As he had throughout the day, Scott held Rachel's hand, serving as her lifeline.

It was only when they climbed aboard the small commuter plane, that he relinquished his hold on her, and then only by necessity, for the aisle was barely wide enough for one person. There was no question of sitting next to each other, for the plane boasted only one seat on each side, but once the other passengers were seated, Scott reached across the aisle and captured Rachel's hand once more.

They sat silently through the flight, as though they had exhausted themselves making conversation while Danny was in surgery, and were now content to simply gaze at each other. Rachel noted that, although he smiled, Scott looked haggard. The effort he had made to cheer the three of them had taken its toll.

"Thanks for coming with me," she said softly when they were in the car, heading for home. "I don't know what I would have done without you."

Scott turned to look at her. "You'd have managed."

His tone was matter-of-fact, denying the magnitude of what he had done.

"Probably," Rachel agreed, "but it helped a lot having you there. I won't say that I worried less, but it didn't seem as scary, because you were sharing my fears." She placed her hand on his, trying to show him just how much he had helped.

"I'm glad." This time Scott's voice was low but fervent. "That's what marriage is all about, isn't it? Sharing the good times and the bad ones."

Rachel nodded slowly. When she had married Scott, it had been for only one reason: saving Danny. Today they accomplished that. Thanks to the surgery, there was no need for the marriage to continue beyond the year Grandma's will stipulated. She ought to be thrilled. Instead, that thought filled her with sadness, for Rachel could not deny Scott's assertion that they shared much more than a house.

"Do you mind if we stop at the station?" Scott asked as they approached the center of town. "I want to tell Luke the news in person. He knows how worried we've been."

They ran into the station, holding hands and grinning like people who had won the lottery.

"Fantastic!" Luke raised his fists in a salute of happiness. "Didn't I tell you Danny was one tough kid?"

They talked for a few minutes, telling Luke what they knew of the surgery. When Rachel turned to walk back to the car, Luke put a hand on Scott's shoulder. "I don't want to rain on your parade, but I figure you ought to know. You got a FedEx package from the agency today."

Rachel could feel Scott's tension. In all likelihood,

this was the answer he'd been dreading, the decision about his storage tanks. A sinking feeling settled in her stomach. She had been too late. Art hadn't had time to reach his contacts at the agency before the decision was made. Now their only hope would be to appeal it.

As Luke handed the cardboard envelope to Scott, Rachel hurried to his side and put her arm around his waist. Though she couldn't do anything to change the contents of the package, perhaps her touch would comfort him as his had done for her during Danny's surgery.

Scott ripped the tab and pulled out the packet of paper. Rachel watched as his eyes scanned the first page, then moved back to the top to read it carefully. And as he read, his look of cautious optimism changed to pure joy.

"We did it!" he cried, wrapping his arms around Rachel and whirling her in a circle. "The agency approved the permits." He whirled her again before setting her back on the ground. "Luke, where's the champagne?"

Luke clapped him on the shoulder, then disappeared into the station. Returning a minute later, he handed Rachel and Scott cans of Coke. "It's as close to champagne as we've got," he said. Popping the tab on his, he clinked his can to Scott's and Rachel's. "Here's to a fantastic day!"

For the second time that day, Rachel found herself close to tears of happiness.

"Let's go home, Mrs. Sanders." Scott swallowed the last of his Coke and took her hand. "We're going to celebrate. How about I buy you the finest meal Canela has to offer?"

"At the Sonic?" Rachel tossed him the challenge.

"Why not?"

The house was cool and dark, fragrant with the roses Rachel had cut the previous day. As they entered the front hall, Scott drew Rachel into his arms. His eyes met hers, and the happiness she saw reflected in them was so strong it made her pulse race. Was she seeing Scott's happiness or her own? Somehow, though she had never expected it, she had fallen in love with the man she married.

As she took another step toward him, she brushed against the console table, knocking the nearest object to the floor. It landed with a jangle of metal on marble.

Bemused, Rachel looked down. She had dropped Becky's house keys.

"The dog!" she cried. "I forgot Doxy!"

Chapter Fourteen

W hat a day! It seemed there was no end to the good news. First there had been Danny's surgery, then the permit approvals, and soon Rachel would be home, presumably with news of the puppies. That would give them one more thing to celebrate.

Scott pushed the channel advance button. Surely there had to be something worth watching on TV tonight. But though the cable company boasted 100 channels, not one piqued his interest. Tonight Scott had only one thought: Rachel. If everything went the way he hoped, tonight would mark the true beginning of their marriage, and Rachel would be his wife in more than name.

Scott propped his boots on the table and leaned back, thinking. Rachel had changed. When he had first seen her, sitting in her jaunty red Mustang stranded by the side of the road, he had noticed the superficial changes. The girl he'd known in high school had matured; her clothing was different; her hairstyle spoke of expensive salons; her makeup was skillfully applied. But living with her, particularly the last few weeks, had shown Scott that the changes were more than skin deep. Rachel had grown into a compassionate, caring woman, the woman he wanted to spend the rest of his life with, the woman he wanted for his wife—his real wife.

With a groan of frustration, Scott jumped to his feet and began to pace the floor. He had planned to wait until the year was over before he told her, but plans, Scott had learned, were made to be revised. Only a saint could continue living the way he was, and Scott was no saint. He couldn't continue the charade, pretending that the only reason he had married her was for the money. It was time to talk to Rachel, to tell her the truth. And then . . . if everything went according to plan, there would be no need for words, at least not for a long time.

Unable to concentrate on the television, Scott wandered into the kitchen. If Rachel spent much more time at her sister's house, there wouldn't be much evening left. She might not want to eat out, even at the Sonic. Scott opened the freezer and peered at the contents. Good. It might not be gourmet, but he could make Rachel one of his freezer cuisine dinners. That way they wouldn't starve.

He pulled several cardboard boxes from the freezer and plunked them onto the counter. A nice tossed salad would add one of those fruit and vegetable servings Rachel thought were so important. They could even have strawberry sundaes instead of hot fudge. That would add more nutrition. And hadn't he read somewhere that strawberries were an aphrodisiac?

Maybe Rachel's insistence on fruit servings wasn't such a bad idea.

As he walked toward the small pantry, Scott noticed the red light flashing on the answering machine. Though his first response was to ignore it, Scott realized Becky or Tim might have called with updated information about Danny. He hit the playback button.

"Rachel, it's Art. Give me a call about your husband's permits."

At first, the meaning of the message didn't register. A second later, it hit him and a haze of hurt confusion descended over him. His vision blurred so that the only thing he saw was the red light, blinking more slowly now, taunting him, reminding him that nothing had changed.

How could she have done it? Scott wasn't sure what was worse, Rachel's meddling or the fact that she had betrayed him. All he knew was that nothing, nothing in his life, had hurt this much. The Marines had taught him to endure physical pain, but no amount of training could have prepared him for this.

Rachel was just like his mother. Scott clenched his fists, then forced himself to relax. Rachel would try to justify her actions; he knew that. But it wouldn't work. No matter what she might say, she was interfering, trying to run his life as if he were a child, incapable of doing anything himself.

How often would he have to tell her that the station was his—his alone—and that he would make a success of it by himself? Scott thought he had made that perfectly clear, but Rachel hadn't listened. No, she had to intercede just the way his mother had, calling Coach Brown after the tryouts and asking him to put Scott on the football team, even though he hadn't made the grade.

That had been humiliating; the other boys had learned of the call and had teased Scott mercilessly. But this was worse. It would have been bad enough if Rachel had called the agency. But worse, she called that crook of a lawyer she used to work for.

Scott stormed upstairs. He had to get out of here, away from this house, its memories and—most of all—its broken dreams. There was no doubt that the dream he had harbored for so long, the one that kept him awake most nights, would never come true.

He wanted the permits. There was no question about that. And he would have done almost anything to get them approved. Almost anything *legal*, that is. But he would never have gone beyond the limits of honesty to get them. It would be better to see the station languish than to do something dishonest. That was the difference between him and the woman he had married, the woman he thought he knew.

They had reached the end of the line. Though he couldn't return the permits, he could make sure that this never, ever happened again.

It was getting to be a habit, singing in the car. She could have whistled or hummed, but somehow nothing short of singing seemed an appropriate expression of her happiness. Rachel couldn't remember when she had felt so happy. Any way you looked at it, today had been a perfect day.

Without a doubt, the most important thing was Danny's surgery, with the permits in second place, but Doxy's puppies were the icing on the cake. The dachshund had been lying in her bed with three little balls of fur lined up on one side of their mother, drinking greedily. Rachel knew better than to try to touch the puppies and had contented herself with snapping pictures for Danny, but oh, how her fingers had ached to hold one of the pups.

"Scott, wait until you see them." Rachel tossed her keys on the kitchen counter and rushed into the hallway. She had to see Scott, to share the latest wonder with him. "They're just the cutest things imaginable. Danny'll be so excited when he sees them."

There was no answer. Rachel looked into the den. It was empty. So was the parlor, and all the rooms, even the kitchen.

"Scott, where are you?"

Still no answer. A prickle of fear began to dissolve her euphoria. The whole first floor seemed empty. Scott might be upstairs, but why hadn't he answered her calls?

She climbed the stairs two at a time. Light spilled from Scott's room onto the hallway floor.

"Scott?" Rachel stood in the doorway, suddenly speechless, for Scott had dumped the contents of his dresser drawers onto the bed and was stuffing shirts and pants into a duffel bag.

"What are you doing?" she asked.

Scott didn't bother to look up. Instead he grabbed two tee shirts and wadded them into balls before he tossed them into the duffel. "What does it look like I'm doing?" His voice was harsh, totally devoid of the tender tone it held when he had promised to buy her dinner. Had that been only an hour ago?

"It looks like you've entered some sort of wrinkled clothes contest," Rachel said.

At that, Scott raised his head. "Real funny, Rachel. Ha, ha." His words fairly dripped with sarcasm. "You always did have a sense of humor."

Something was very, very wrong, but Rachel had no clue to the cause. "What happened?"

Scott pummeled the contents of the duffel bag as he tried to force another pair of jeans into it. "You'll have to excuse me," he said in a deceptively calm voice, "if I'm not in the mood for polite conversation." He stood up, straightening his back and shoulders. It was probably instinctive, the result of his years in the Marine Corps. Even if not deliberate, the stance was definitely intimidating. Where was the gentle man who held her while she cried, the man who kept her spirits from plummeting during Danny's surgery? Where was the man she loved?

Scott zipped the duffel and slung it over his shoulder. "Just get out of my way."

For a second Rachel didn't move. This wasn't happening. It couldn't be happening. But as Scott took a step toward the door, she knew he wasn't joking. "Where are you going?"

Scott shook his head. "It doesn't matter. The simple fact is, I'm leaving."

Leaving? Rachel blinked in confusion. "Why?"

"Let's just say that I came to my senses. I don't want you, and I don't want your money."

Rachel could feel the blood drain from her face. He sounded serious. He *was* serious. But why? "Scott, I don't understand. I was only gone a few minutes. What happened?"

"The permits, Rachel. That's what happened."

The world had turned upside down. That was the only explanation Rachel could imagine for Scott's behavior. "Your permits were approved," she said, still bewildered by his words and actions. "Why are you so upset?"

"The innocent act won't work with me." Scott's words were little more than a snarl. "Don't even try to deny that you called that crook, Art Langston."

Scott's boots clattered as he raced down the stairs. Rachel followed, gripping the banister to keep from tripping as she tried to match her husband's pace.

How had he learned about her call? She hadn't told Scott, and no one else knew. Rachel hadn't told Becky or even Mary of her efforts to expedite the permitting process. "Of course I called him, but—"

"I have no time for 'buts.' It's over, Rachel. The charade's over."

As the front door closed behind Scott, Rachel felt her knees begin to buckle. He wasn't joking; Scott had left her, and she had no idea why. Nothing made sense. His permits had been approved; he'd been thrilled; they'd planned to celebrate. And now, this.

Her throat dry with fear, Rachel walked toward the kitchen. As she switched on the overhead light, she saw the blinking light on the answering machine. Thirty seconds later, Rachel understood how Scott had learned of her call to Art, but she still didn't understand why that call had upset him.

She poured a glass of water and forced herself to take slow sips. When she had emptied the glass, she had regained a small measure of composure, enough to realize that she needed to talk to someone. Becky had enough worries of her own without Rachel bothering her, and she could hardly expect Luke to answer her questions about his boss and good friend.

Mary. She would visit Mary.

Visiting hours had ended by the time Rachel arrived at Magnolia Gardens, and so she went directly to the administrator's office. Mrs. Nelson was normally an accommodating person; she would probably agree to let Rachel see Mary.

"I know it's late, but. . . ."

Mrs. Nelson rose and stretched out a hand to Rachel. "You got here sooner than I'd thought. I hope you didn't speed too much."

"You were expecting me?" Rachel shook her head as though to clear the cobwebs. Since she had seen Doxy's puppies, nothing had been normal. Perhaps she had fallen through some crack into the "Twilight Zone." That might explain first Scott's and now Mrs. Nelson's unexpected behavior.

The administrator seemed equally perplexed. "Then you didn't get my message?"

Rachel shook her head. "I was hoping you'd let me visit Mary tonight, even though it's late."

Mrs. Nelson's eyes closed briefly. When she opened them, she gestured toward one of the chairs in front of her desk. "Sit down, my dear." When Rachel complied, she said, "There's no easy way to say this. I called to tell you that Mary died about two o'clock this afternoon."

The image of a hospital clock flashed before Rachel's eyes. That had been the time when Dr. Martin had come out of the operating room, announcing that Danny's surgery had been successful.

"No!" Her cry was instinctive. "It can't be true."

Mrs. Nelson nodded. "She knew her time was near. For the past week or so, she's been putting her affairs in order."

Rachel remembered the last time she had seen Mary; the older woman had said she was tired and had asked Rachel to stay until she fell asleep. That was unlike Mary. And then there had been the day Mary learned of Becky's pregnancy, when she had said something about making room for the baby. At the time, Rachel had thought she meant furnishing a new nursery, but maybe she had meant room of a different kind.

"I still can't believe she's gone." Rachel started to cry. "Mary was my friend."

Mrs. Nelson pushed a box of tissues toward Rachel. "And you were hers," she said. "I know how much she treasured your visits."

The words were meant to comfort, and perhaps in time they would. But for the moment Rachel felt nothing but a sense of loss and emptiness. She was alone. Her perfect day had turned into a nightmare.

Chapter Fifteen

It was not the best night of her life. In fact, it was one of the worst. The only good thing she could say what that by some miracle she had gotten home from Magnolia Gardens without causing an accident. How she'd done that with tears streaming down her face, and her mind picturing Mary's sweet smile rather than stop signs, was one of life's mysteries.

Once home Rachel flung herself onto her bed and cried until there were no tears left—cried for Mary, for Scott and for her own lost dreams. She had lost far more than a friend. Scott's words had made it clear that their relationship and any hope of a future together were gone, *kaput, fini,* over. When at last she fell asleep, it was a restless sleep, filled with nightmares where she was being pursued by faceless, nameless horrors. With the dawn, daylight changed the nightmares into reality. Rachel was able to give her fears a name: life without Scott.

She pulled on a robe, then stumbled downstairs. Though she wasn't looking forward to making the call, common courtesy demanded it. Rachel poured her first cup of coffee and picked up the phone.

"I wish all my cases were as easy as this one," Art Langston said when Rachel thanked him for interceding on Scott's behalf. "I'd like to take credit, but the fact is, I didn't do anything. By the time I reached my contact at the agency, he said the permits had already been approved."

Rachel gripped her mug with both hands and stared at the dark liquid as though the answers to her questions might be found in its depth. The news ought to have pleased her, for it meant that Scott had obtained the permits the way he wanted to: with no outside assistance. If only it were that simple! But where Scott was concerned, little was simple.

In the long hours before she fell asleep, Rachel replayed Scott's parting scene in her mind, picturing the anger on his face, hearing his hurtful words. And as she relived those ugly moments, Rachel realized that, even though Scott might believe it, the permits weren't the cause of his anger. They were nothing more than a catalyst. Something deeper had caused Scott's outburst, something that had been festering for weeks, if not months.

The problem was Rachel didn't know what that something could be. Perhaps it was an aspect of their marriage, or something rooted in his years in the Marine Corps, or even a vestige of his childhood. Though she was ashamed to admit it, she lived with Scott, she loved him, but she didn't understand him.

Carrying a mug of coffee in one hand, Rachel started toward the stairs. It was time to dress and check on Doxy's puppies.

The door to the parlor was half open. Afterward, Rachel couldn't have said what prompted her to open it rather than slide it closed, but she pushed the pocket door back into the wall. A ray of morning sun spilled through the partially closed drapes, focusing on the piano. Her imagination conjured an image of herself sitting on the piano bench, practicing a Chopin prelude, while Grandma Laura sat next to her, turning pages. It had been Becky who was supposed to help Rachel practice, but her younger sister had complained that Rachel hit too many wrong notes. So Grandma had taken over the responsibility, applauding when Rachel finished a piece, never mentioning the times when Rachel's fingers had fumbled and produced sounds that would have made Chopin cringe. Odd, but she had forgotten those hours that they spent together, hours when Grandma Laura had seemed more like an older sister than a disapproving parent.

Rachel closed the door, a thoughtful expression on her face as she climbed the stairs. She had every intention of going directly to her room, yet her feet seemed to have a will of their own, because she found herself staring at the door to her grandmother's room, her hand on the knob. There was no reason not to open it. It was, after all, only a room, and it did need airing out. As she slid a doorstop under the heavy door, Rachel's eyes were drawn to the bed. Made of dark mahogany with intricately carved legs, Rachel had always considered it a monstrous piece of furniture. And yet today it looked different. This morning, instead of remembering how she had hated dusting the deep grooves, Rachel thought of the week when she had

been home from school, sick with a childhood ill-
nesses.

Though Grandma Laura had had an inviolable rule
that the girls were not allowed in her bed, no matter
how fierce their nightmares had been, no matter how
much their stomachs ached, this time she had allowed
Rachel to sleep in her bed. And when Rachel had
started feeling well enough to eat, Grandma, the
woman who had declared that tables and not beds
were where a person ate, had brought her a cup of
cocoa.

Rachel leaned against the doorframe and closed her
eyes, remembering. She saw her grandmother's face.
It was the same face she had seen every day for fifteen
years, and yet it wasn't. This time, Grandma Laura
was smiling. Gone was the dour, disapproving expression Rachel remembered. In its place was a warm
smile, a loving smile.

Rachel smiled in response, and then her eyes filled
with tears. It was true. Both Mary and Becky had been
right. Her grandmother did love her. The things she
had done, everything from Rachel's birthday cheesecake to cocoa in bed, were her way of saying "I love
you."

Rachel walked slowly into the room, seeing it as if
for the first time. She ran her hand over the chenille
bedspread, surprised at the memories the textured
cloth evoked. What was it about touch? Or was it more
than touch?

Rachel remembered her grandmother declaring that
actions were more powerful than words. Was that because Grandma had been uncomfortable with words?
Rachel didn't know. What she did know was that, had

her grandmother been able to say the words, had she told Rachel she loved her, their lives might have been different. Rachel might not have left Canela. She and her grandmother might not have been estranged. Simple words, and yet they could have changed so much.

The thought hit Rachel with the impact of a blow. Staggering slightly, she gripped the edge of the bed and sank onto it. *She was just like her grandmother.* Rachel shuddered, horrified by the thought. Grandma Laura was not a person she would have chosen as a role model, and yet how could she deny the evidence? She was doing the same thing—making exactly the same mistake—as her grandmother.

Though Rachel loved Scott with all her heart, she had never said the words. She had taken it for granted that he would understand, that he would realize when she planned their night at the drive-in or when she brought him a picnic lunch at the station, she was doing it out of love.

And now it was too late.

Rachel buried her face in her hands. How could she have been so stupid? She had thrown away her hope for happiness.

"Life is too short to waste a minute of it. If you want something, make it happen." Rachel's eyes flew open. Mary's words were so clear that for a moment Rachel thought the older woman was in the room with her. She was alone, and yet she wasn't. Rachel smiled. Though she might never see Mary again, she would never forget her advice. Mary was right.

Maybe, just maybe, it wasn't too late.

* * *

Luke's apartment sure lacked the comforts of home. Stark walls, minimalist furnishings, not even a green plant. Still, beggars couldn't be choosers, and—mindful of the ever active Canela grapevine—Scott hadn't wanted to check into a motel. He had told Luke that Rachel decided to spend the night at Becky's house to be near the new puppies, and that he thought this would be a good chance to catch up on news with his old buddy. It was doubtful Luke believed the tale; even to Scott's ears, it sounded feeble. But at least Luke hadn't questioned him and had offered the dubious comforts of his sofa.

As a sleeping surface, it was definitely deficient, and Scott had done little sleeping, though he could not blame his insomnia on the lumpy couch. Though it was the last thing he wanted to do, Scott had spent the majority of the night replaying the scene in his bedroom, reliving the words he had hurled at Rachel, remembering the reason he had been so angry. It had been a horribly painful night, but as dawn broke, Scott found the anger had dissipated, leaving nothing in its wake but emptiness.

"So, what's it gonna be: premium or regular? Make up your mind." Scott snarled at the woman in the green minivan. Her eyes widened, and she stared at him as if he'd suddenly turned into a vampire.

"Hey, man." Luke strode from the office, gripped Scott's arm and dragged him away from the pumps. "What's going on? You trying to destroy all your hard work in one morning?" he demanded when they were both inside the station. "You're gonna lose customers that way."

Scott shook off Luke's hand. "Butt out." Leaving

Luke to handle the morning customers, he strode into his office and took pleasure from slamming the door behind him.

It was stupid. Scott jerked the chair from under the desk and sank onto it. By all rights, he ought to be happy. After all, he was well on his way to getting everything he wanted, everything he had planned and worked for for so long. Why, then, did he feel nothing but emptiness? He propped his boots on the desk and frowned.

Rachel. It all came back to Rachel.

The station didn't matter. The respect of Canela's townspeople didn't matter. Nothing mattered except Rachel, and nothing—absolutely nothing—mattered without her. Everything else was just a sham, an empty shell. Rachel was his heart, and he had lost her.

Scott looked down at his desk and glared. The FedEx package containing his permits lay in the center, mocking him. He had the permits. He could expand the station. So what? A large, profitable station didn't warm a man's heart or bring laughter to his life. Rachel did.

So what if she had helped get the permits approved? Why was he so hung up on that? Rachel had good intentions. She called Art Langston for one reason and one reason only: she knew how important those blasted permits were to Scott. She wanted to help, and he was an ungrateful fool.

Scott struck his forehead with his fist. What an idiot he was! Even a child knew that there was a difference between helping and controlling, but he'd been too blind to see it. He had once accused Rachel of being self-centered, of seeing things from only her own perspective, and now he'd done exactly the same thing. He never considered her perspective or her motives. Instead, he had lashed out in anger, and in doing that, he had hurt her.

Scott jumped to his feet and began to pace the floor. Would he ever forget the pain on Rachel's face last night—a pain he had caused? How on earth could he have told her he didn't want her? Talk about lies! He wanted her so much that he lay awake most nights, thinking of her, wishing he could be with her. And yet he said he didn't want her.

Stupid.

Rachel would be justified if she refused to ever see him again. She would probably do exactly that. And yet. . . .

Scott grabbed his keys.

The phone rang.

Ten minutes. He would be here in ten minutes. Rachel swallowed, trying to dislodge the lump that rested in her throat. As the time drew near, what had seemed like a good idea two hours before now felt like a mistake. A huge mistake.

Scott hadn't wanted to come. She sensed that. He sounded odd when he answered the phone, as though he had just swallowed a hot liquid and scalded his throat, and when she asked him to come home, he was silent for a moment, probably thinking of a reason to refuse. For what seemed like an eternity, she was sure he *would* refuse. But then he said, "okay." Nothing more.

Everything was ready. He was coming. Now, if only—

She heard his key in the lock, and her hands began to tremble. What would he think? What would he do?

"Scott, I'm in the parlor." By some miracle, her voice betrayed none of her nervousness. Rachel switched on the stereo and slid the pocket door open.

Now! In a few moments she would have his answer.

He stood in the doorway for a moment, his eyes fixed on Rachel. "What on earth?" He sounded astonished.

Rachel smoothed the skirt of her gown in what she knew to be a nervous gesture as she tried to keep a smile on her face. The lump in her throat grew. He didn't like it! It was a gamble; she knew that when she filled the room with flowers, chose the music Scott had played the day they were married and then waited for him, dressed in her wedding gown. She had hoped he would understand.

Rachel shook her head slowly. Would she never learn? She was once again relying on actions when Scott needed words.

Taking a deep breath and exhaling slowly, Rachel tried to relax. "I know we can't start over, Scott," she said in a voice that sounded miraculously calm, "but I want to make a fresh start." His frown disappeared, and now his lips were straight, neither approving nor disapproving.

Rachel swallowed nervously. What if he laughed and told her she was a fool? How could she bear it? And yet, what chance for happiness did she have if she didn't take a chance? No matter what Scott said or did, she had to try.

"I want a real marriage."

"A real marriage?" Scott raised one brow as though he doubted her words.

Rachel nodded. She had known this wouldn't be easy, but she had never dreamt it would be so difficult. "Forever and for children."

He was silent for a long moment before he asked, "Do you really mean that?" Scott's voice was calm, matter-of-fact, making Rachel feel like she was being cross-examined by an attorney.

"More than anything in my life." Despite her best efforts, her voice quavered with emotion. So much depended on Scott's reaction. He said nothing, and for a moment Rachel was tempted to flee, to leave before she bared her soul completely. Rachel felt a moment of sympathy for her grandmother. No wonder Laura hadn't expressed her emotions; the fear of rejection was very real and very powerful.

"I know I've made a lot of mistakes," she said. "I've hurt you, and I'm sorry." Rachel stretched a hand toward him, then dropped it when he made no move to touch her. "I can't promise that I'll never hurt you again, but I can promise that it won't ever be deliberate. Oh, Scott, I don't think any woman—even Justine—could love you as much as I do."

Scott took a quick breath. "You love me?" There was a sense of wonder in his voice, and Rachel saw a gleam of something—could it be hope?—in his eyes.

"More than I ever dreamed possible." She fixed her gaze on his, willing him to believe her. "I don't want to live without you, and I don't want to give you back to Justine."

Scott smiled, a smile so full of happiness that it

warmed Rachel's heart. He took two steps toward her and took her hands in his. "Sweetheart," he said with an odd smile, "there is no Justine."

The words were so unexpected that all Rachel could do was stare. No Justine?

"I invented her."

As Rachel shook her head, the scent of roses filled her nostrils, their sweetness reminding her of the nights she had walked in the garden rather than listen to Scott's conversations with Justine. "Scott, I heard you on the phone with her."

He chuckled. "I was talking to a dial tone. That's why you never saw the charges on your phone bill. Talk about feeling stupid! There I was, holding a phone in my hand, talking to a phantom woman and telling her all the things I wanted to say to you."

Rachel remembered how she had blushed at some of the things she'd heard Scott murmur. "All those romantic words were for me?"

Scott nodded and tightened his grip on her hands. "Rachel, I've loved you since we were in school. I knew you didn't love me, so I used to tell myself that you just weren't ready." Scott's shrug was a deprecating one. "The main reason I came back to Canela was the hope of seeing you again."

Rachel stared, wanting to believe him and yet not trusting her ears. Scott loved her? Was it possible that her dreams could come true? Scott smiled, and she could no longer doubt that what she saw shining in his eyes was love. Scott loved her!

"When I heard about your grandmother's will, I couldn't believe my luck. I had the chance to marry the woman I loved."

She wanted to believe it. Oh, how she wanted to believe it! "But you told me it was a business arrangement. You said you needed the money."

"I lied."

That was a good story, but Rachel wasn't convinced. "You applied for a loan. Everyone knew that."

"Exactly." Scott nodded. "That's why I did it. I wanted you to think I really needed the money. What you don't know is that I saw a lawyer before we were married. He set up an irrevocable trust, leaving all the money to you." Rachel remembered the day she had seen Scott entering an attorney's office. Was that why he was there? As if he heard her unspoken question, Scott said, "I never wanted there to be any question that I would have married you if you had been bankrupt."

A weight she hadn't known was there lifted from Rachel's heart. "I still don't understand about Justine. Why did you invent her?"

"Protection." Scott moved a step closer to Rachel. "One of the lessons I learned in the Marines was to plan ahead and avoid combat situations." Rachel smiled at the thought that marriage was a combat situation. "I couldn't let you know how vulnerable my heart was. Justine was my barricade to keep you from getting close to the truth."

Rachel nodded. She could understand that. Hadn't she done the same thing herself, trying to keep her heart whole?

"I've been in a lot of tough situations over the years," Scott continued, "but the hardest thing I've ever done is live with you. Rachel, it's been terrible living here as your friend, not being able to tell you I love you,"

Rachel's smile was radiant. "That's over. The charade is ended." She looked at her wedding gown, and for the first time she felt like a bride, filled with love. "From now on, we have a real marriage. No strings attached."

Scott laughed. In one swift movement, he swept her into his arms.